"YOU GENTS LOOKING FOR A LEAD BELLY?"

Slocum reached into the box and extracted his Winchester, levered a shell in and then swung the muzzle around. He held the gun's butt to his hip, and his action forced them to stop in the middle of the road.

"Where are you going with that lumber?" the pot-bellied man with the mustache asked.

"Guess the same place where you're going."

"We've got the only contract to haul that up there to Owl Creek."

"Free country, boys," Slocum replied. "I'm taking a lady some lumber she needs. Anyone want to stop me, step forward for his bullet."

DON'T MISS THESE
ALL-ACTION WESTERN SERIES
FROM THE BERKLEY PUBLISHING GROUP

THE GUNSMITH by J. R. Roberts
    Clint Adams was a legend among lawmen, outlaws, and ladies.
    They called him . . . the Gunsmith.

LONGARM by Tabor Evans
    The popular long-running series about U.S. Deputy Marshal
    Long—his life, his loves, his fight for justice.

SLOCUM by Jake Logan
    Today's longest-running action Western. John Slocum rides a
    deadly trail of hot blood and cold steel.

BUSHWHACKERS by B. J. Lanagan
    An action-packed series by the creators of Longarm! The rousing
    adventures of the most brutal gang of cutthroats ever assembled—
    Quantrill's Raiders.

JAKE LOGAN

SLOCUM AND THE MINER'S JUSTICE

JOVE BOOKS, NEW YORK

SLOCUM AND THE MINER'S JUSTICE

A Jove Book / published by arrangement with
the author

PRINTING HISTORY
Jove edition / October 1998

The Penguin Putnam Inc. World Wide Web site address is
http://www.penguinputnam.com

ISBN: 0-515-12371-4

A JOVE BOOK®
Jove Books are published by The Berkley Publishing Group,
a member of Penguin Putnam Inc.,
200 Madison Avenue, New York, New York 10016.
JOVE and the "J" design are trademarks
belonging to Jove Publications, Inc.

PRINTED IN THE UNITED STATES OF AMERICA

10 9 8 7 6 5 4 3 2 1

Prologue

Some folks called 1878 the start of the New Bonanza Era. Democrats controlled both houses of Congress for the first time in over three decades, and despite the veto of the Bland-Allison Act by President Rutherford Hayes, the Congress overrode him. The new legislation required the U.S. Treasury to buy four million dollars worth of silver bullion each year for coinage. And the shouts of hurrah could be heard from the mining towns in Montana to the Mexican border. Gold and silver prices hit new highs overnight, and a big rush was on to find the still-undiscovered mother lodes all over the West.

1

Owl Creek Camp, Arizona Territory, March 15, 1878

The sounds of hammers and hand saws shattered the thin mountain air. A few puffs of white clouds hung around the purple peaks of the Bradshaw Mountains, which towered over the valley. Campfire smoke swirled close to the ground on the cool wind that swept out of the north. At intervals, ear-shattering blasts of dynamite echoed off the pine-clad slopes and made Slocum's dun horse shy at their reports.

Slocum reined up his mount, and then he twisted in the saddle to take in all the activity in the valley. Twenty feet below the road, in the surging creek, several men stood in the swirling water and scooped up gravel and sand to dump into their makeshift sluices. They barely glanced up and acknowledged him before they returned to their furious labor.

Obviously, this whole valley was on fire with a gold strike. Slocum wondered whether he would find Buster Markley anywhere in the camp. Markley had taken all the proceeds from the sale of the saloon that they had jointly owned in Silver City, New Mexico Territory. There was no way that Markley would be doing any manual work like those rough-dressed miners in that icy water. The stream had to be cold, for it came from melted snow on those peaks above him. Slocum shivered under his brown suit coat; the wind alone was chilly enough, after spending all winter down in the warm desert around his mining claim in the Tombstone district. Realizing he'd have to search the camp for Markley, he pushed his horse on to the cluster of tents and half-finished buildings ahead.

He dropped his lanky frame heavily from the saddle in front of a white canvas tent. A hand-painted sign hung on the tent's peak and said, "Eats Here." He tied his horse at the fresh-peeled hitch rack. The flaps of the tent were open, and he could see inside. There were white-checkered table-cloths on rough board tables lined with benches on both sides of them.

When he entered, a handsome woman in her late twenties looked up in the back portion of the tent with her arms elbow-deep in a wooden tub of soapy dishwater. She nodded, then brushed a wisp of her light brown hair back from her face with the side of her hand. She had a full figure, and wore a prim blue dress with a starched white apron over it. She quit the dishes, straightened, and then dried her hands.

"Be right with you," she said.

"No rush. I haven't eaten in two days."

"That long?" she asked as if taken aback by what he had said. Then she stared hard at him with green eyes that sought the truth of his situation.

"Maybe I had some crackers and cheese during that time," Slocum said, "but mind you, they were old and stale, ma'am." He held his hat in his hands.

"Well, I'm kinda past serving breakfast and lunch isn't ready yet. I could fry you up some elk steaks and throw in some cold biscuits left over from this morning with a little gravy I'd rustle up. But I'd only go to that much trouble for a starving man." She gave him another hard questioning look.

"I'd sure be that man. Sounds wonderful, if you've got time to mess with me."

"Oh, you look like an honest enough sort of fella. I'll do it." She paused as if considering him. "You ain't struck it rich now, have you?"

"What do you mean?' "

"Mean? My gawd, man, that's what this camp is all about. Getting rich. Can't you see all of this construction going on? Why, I'm cooking on a campfire out back until some of them carpenters can find time and build me a kitchen out there. And I'm paying two dollars a burro-load for stove wood. Can you believe that?"

"Oh, yes, ma'am. I'd have sure been blind not to have seen the rush going on. Has anyone found a good vein yet?"

"Well, you can hear anything. You know how miners go on. But I expect there will be several."

"Good. You don't know a man calls himself Buster Markley who might be up here?"

"No." She cupped her elbow in one hand and squeezed her firm chin with the other hand as if in deep thought. "I know most of the men around town, but I never heard of him. You looking for him?"

"Yes, ma'am. He owes me some money."

"Excuse me, my name's Hap Arnold. That's short for Happiness." She stuck out her hand and he shook it.

"Nice to meet you, Mrs. Arnold." Her fingers felt strong and callused in his grasp; this woman knew work and used them.

"Hap's good enough. Mr. Arnold run off a while back, and I've been happy ever since." She smiled at him.

"He must have lost his senses, leaving you. Slocum's my name," he said. They released their handshake, and he put his hat on the bench.

"Joe Arnold never had any sense that I could tell. I should have listened to my mother. She told me not to marry him." She motioned Slocum to take a seat. "I'll pour you some coffee and then you can drink it while I go out back and rustle up your grub.''

"If you ain't opposed to my company, I'll come along and watch. Besides, you can fill me in on the gold rush around here.''

She poured a crockery cup of steaming coffee, and then handed it to him.

"Not much to tell you so far,'' she said, setting the blue granite pot back on the small cast-iron stove. "I was down at Wickenburg when they came in my cafe one day yelling that they'd struck gold and lots of it up in the Bradshaws.''

"So?'' he asked, holding the cup up to blow on the liquid as they stepped out behind her tent.

She squatted down and stirred up the fire under her iron grates, then took a skillet from the box beside her and put it on the grates. With grace, she rose to her feet again, and went to a tarp-covered wagon. On the tailgate, she unwrapped an elk quarter, sliced off a few thick steaks, and then rewrapped it in the canvas wrapping.

"Pretty fat one for this early,'' she said, showing the meat to him and then going back to the fire.

"Looks good enough for me. So you heard about the gold strike?''

"Yeah, well, with Joe off chasing his dreams . . . I guess he went looking for gold too last fall. He never said he was leaving. He never come back neither.'' She busied herself placing the meat in the pan to fry, and then with a hook lifted the lid on a Dutch oven.

"Here, catch,'' she said, and tossed him a brown biscuit. "That should stave off your appetite for a little while.''

"It will. Thanks,'' he said, and began to eat.

"Anyway, I sold my cafe down there, loaded all my things in a wagon, and come up here to get rich myself.''

"Hap! Hap! Come quick. They've brought in Charlie McRoy and he's bad hurt. Been shot.''

She rose to her feet, looking at the steaks on the grill,

and then at the flush-faced young man who was waiting out of breath, in the opening of the tent.

"I'm kind of the doc up here too," she explained to Slocum.

"Go see about him," Slocum said. "I'll watch this unless you need me."

"You watch that," she said, and rushed off with the young man. "I'll be back quick as I can. There's more biscuits in that Dutch oven. Help yourself."

When the two of them were gone, Slocum studied the pine slopes that rose above the camp. Someone had no doubt jumped a claim or robbed a miner. It was the same story everywhere he went—greed and gold ran in the same vein. There would be plenty more of the same trouble in this valley. There was no visible law and no one responsible for it, most likely. He closed his eyelids as the wind shifted and the sharp wood smoke swept over his face and made his eyes smart.

He took the hook and removed the Dutch oven's lid. The first sourdough biscuit had drawn the saliva into his mouth, and another one wouldn't hurt. He chewed on it slowly, and then washed it down with what was left of his coffee while the elk sizzled in the pan.

When the meat was cooked, he placed it and a few more of her biscuits on a plate, then went back inside to eat. He had set his dish of food on the table and started for another cup of coffee when he saw her enter the tent.

"Couldn't save him," she said crestfallen, and collapsed on the bench opposite his plate. For a second, she buried her face in her arms. "He'd lost a lot of blood and was in bad shape. Nice old man—he knew this country real well and he knew gold." She shook her head.

"You want some coffee?" he asked, holding up an empty cup.

"Sure. I could use some whiskey instead."

"I've got some out in my saddlebags." He tossed his thumb in that direction.

"Oh, no." She smiled at his offer, and then dismissed it. "I was only talking."

"I've sure got it if you want it."

"Been on two toots in my whole life," she said. "One night I got word that Joe was drunk and at some house— you know what kind I mean? We hadn't been married very long. I started feeling sorry for myself, and then I found a quart of rye in the cupboard. Man, a few drinks of that and I was ready. Took one of Joe's old cap-and-ball pistols up there to that whorehouse, walked right in like I owned the place, and went to shooting the hell out of that fancy chandelier.

"This old heifer owned the place—you've probably seen the kind. She had this real low-cut silk dress and came screaming down the stairs telling me to quit—how that chandelier use to belong to Jefferson Davis.

" 'Well, by gawd, Joe Arnold use to belong to me too, sister,' I said, all drunk out of my head, weaving on my heels, and ready to snap off another one at that shining glassware over my head.

" 'I'm sending him home right now!' she shouted. 'Don't fire another shot.' Then she flew back up them stairs.

" 'You better hurry,' I warned her.

"Next thing I knew she was back; she had Joe by the ear, him in his underwear, and his clothes in her other hand. Kind of embarrassing. She marched him down the stairs and gave him to me. Oh, I recall that man's scathing remarks.

" 'You have embarrassed me in public,' he raged like some offended gentleman.

" 'See this gun?' I shoved the barrel up his nose to get his attention. 'Next time that I hear that you are in one of these houses, I won't come shoot no damn Confederate lights out. I'm coming to kill you. You savvy that, Joe?' "

"What happened the second time you got drunk?" Slocum asked, cutting off another piece of the tender elk.

She shook her head and then dropped her chin as if unable to tell him. "You won't want to hear about it."

"I might. I won't know till I've heard it."

"We were taking some saddle horses to a man lived up on the Verde River. Joe had been nipping the bottle all day and I swear, I had gathered them horses that day out of the greasewood ten hundred times by myself, him too drunk to hardly ride.

"Well, we made camp on the river that night. He went to sleep before I finished cooking supper. I was so damn mad, I found every pint bottle he had hid and I drank them all."

"What happened?"

"I went swimming . . . stark naked in the river. Whooping and hollering like an Injun on the prowl. Then I drug him in, clothes and all, and about drowned him. Man, it was fun. If anyone had come by and seen us, they'd a figured we both were plumb crazy. Had me a real bad headache the next day, and I swore I'd never drink again all the way up there and back." She shook her head and then swept her hair back from her face with both hands.

"Joe swore too." She paused as if considering the fact. "But he reneged on his word. You ever done anything crazy drunk?"

"Not as funny as that. What do I owe you for the food?" he asked.

"Nothing." She wrinkled her straight nose as if to dismiss the notion.

"Come on, let me pay you."

"There is one thing I'd sure like to have done."

"What's that?"

"Could you make old McRoy a coffin? The guys that eat here would pitch some money in on it, I'm sure."

"I'd have to borrow some tools."

"Wiley next door is building a saloon. He'd loan them to you."

"And boards?"

"You can buy them from Old Man Kramer. He has the monopoly on the lumber business up here. You can't miss him—he has stacks of it on the corner. They come from the sawmill at Prescott. He freights them in here. Here, I've got money to pay for them." She went to digging in her apron pocket.

"I'm sure I have enough to buy some boards. How tall was McRoy?"

"Oh, five-five, I'd say." She held her hand out flat at her shoulders as if to indicate the dead man's height.

"Wiley next door has tools and Kramer has the lumber?" Slocum repeated to confirm it with her.

"Yes. Do you have the time?" she asked.

"Sure," he assured her.

He found Wiley busy driving nails, putting up the porch rafters of the saloon. And when Slocum spoke to him, the older man climbed down his homemade ladder and shook his hand.

"I need to build a coffin for this Charlie McRoy that was shot today. Since I had some time, Hap asked me to do it."

"You want to carpenter, stay here. I could sure use you." The man's blue eyes twinkled at the notion that Slocum might take his offer.

"No." Slocum held his hands up defensively. "I told her I'd make a casket for the dead man is all."

"I'll help you," Wiley said. "Josh," he called, "I'll be right back. Need to go get some boards."

A balding man with a handlebar mustache shouted, "All right!" from the doorway, and Slocum and Wiley marched up to the corner. The lumber was rough-cut and high-priced. Old Man Kramer showed no interest in cutting his prices for a coffin, but for two dollars they soon had enough on their shoulders to make the box.

"I've got the nails," Wiley said as they came back, each one shouldering half of the boards.

They piled them on the new porch, and with the smell of pitch strong in his nose, Slocum shed his coat and took up a pencil and measure to mark the boards. A rectangular box would do. He did not plan to widen it at the arms and narrow it at the head and feet. Wiley took up the saw and went to cutting on the marks.

His partner came outside to see what they were doing, and then nodded when he was told it was for the dead man. He helped nail it together. Soon the box and top were completed. Slocum thanked both men, tossed his jacket over his shoulder, and realized that lunch was being served at Hap's place next door.

She was in a fury passing out bowls of stew to the men crowding the serving table and talking full force. He watched them politely tease her as she served them. A miner with a white towel in his hand was filling coffee cups on the table as fast as he could. As Slocum entered, she looked up at him.

He nodded to indicate the coffin was completed. She acknowledged it with a smile, and then rushed off for more bowls of food.

In no hurry, he found a place on the end of a bench, hitched his holster around to be more comfortable, and then took a seat and decided to wait out noontime rush so he could talk more with her afterwards. There was no sign of Markley in the lunch crowd. Obviously he wasn't around this camp, or Hap would have heard of him. Maybe Slocum would try Crown King next.

In a few seconds she came back, delivering platters of steaming biscuits to her patient customers. Then she nodded to a man's request for another helping. The bowl was passed over the miners' heads, and she took it out back to refill.

"You ain't eating?" the older man across from Slocum asked.

"I ate kinda late today."

"Sure a bad deal about that old Charlie getting shot, huh?" the young man on his right said.

"Bad deal."

"Shame the law ain't up here. Been five men killed in the last month up here in this camp. No one's done a thing."

"You lying devil!" someone shouted outside, and Slocum figured two men out in front of the tent were going to fight. Though he could not see them, he could hear the whack of their blows on each other. Fistfights were a way of life with miners; obviously some of them would rather fight than eat, or they'd have both been inside the tent.

At the report of a gun Slocum rose in haste, then charged past the startled men seated in the tent. Out front, standing in the street over a downed man at his feet, a tall miner in overalls with a black beard and a smoking six-gun in his hand glanced up at Slocum. He snapped off a wild shot over Slocum's head, and Slocum ducked down instinctively, giving the shooter enough time to jump on his dun and ride off unscathed.

Gun in hand, Slocum rushed downhill on his boot heels after the man. Seeing him racing off on his horse, Slocum considered blasting him out of the saddle, but the road was crowded and he had second thoughts. No sense in taking a chance on killing an innocent person. Grim-faced, he spun the cylinder around until the hammer fell on an empty chamber. Then he holstered the Colt.

"Yarby never had a chance, boys," one of the first to examine the body said as he straightened up. "Why, he didn't even have a gun on him. Boys, that's pure murder."

"Yeah!" went up a chorus.

"That killer's name was Stubben," another miner declared. "Shame he killed that young guy."

"It is, but worse than that, boys," Slocum said, disgusted to the core. He pushed his hat up with his thumb. His boots set apart, he stared down the valley where the man had fled. "Stubben stole my good dun horse."

2

Harvey Burns used a penknife to clean the dirt from under his fingernails. Seated in the large chair, he leaned back and considered the entire valley from his vantage point on the hillside in the grove of spindly pines. One day he'd control the entire basin. Let those fools down there root like hogs. In the end, he'd own or control all of it anyway.

Burns was a big man, and his striped pants and black frock coat were fresh-pressed. The frilly white shirt shone in the sun. A saucy magpie scolded him from the pine tree overhead. For a long moment, he considered blasting it off the bough with his .44. There had been a shot down in camp not very long before. From his high vantage point above the camp where, sometime in the future, he intended to build a mansion, he couldn't see where the shot had come from, but it had been near that Arnold woman's tent. He recalled looking hard at her full body several times— she might not be bad in bed.

He'd sure be glad when they finished his saloon down in camp and he had a roof over his head. This business of living in a tent wasn't for him.

"Darling," Lucy drawled, coming from the wall tent that

12

they shared as their living quarters and his office.

He looked up as she strode toward him like a prancing filly. She was dressed in only a corset and pink silk bloomers, and he searched around to be sure no one saw her. That girl sure didn't like to wear clothes. Was that why he kept her? No, he knew why he kept her—she liked it. He'd had his share of whiny bitches, always complaining how their backs hurt or that something was wrong whenever he wanted them in bed. He leaned back in the chair satisfied she was one of a kind. Not bad-looking, reddish-brown hair. If she stayed out in the sun too long, she got freckles on the tops of her breasts where they were exposed. It made her angry too. She must have bought ten jars of vanishing cream to get rid of them.

Hell, those freckles never bothered *him*. He thought they were cute.

"Yes?" he asked, wondering what was wrong.

"That Chinese girl that you hired hasn't shown up today."

"I'll send Mick to find her. She may be working on the side down there." He laughed at the notion of the skinny-ass Oriental girl prostituting herself with the grubby miners.

"I really liked her," Lucy said, taking a seat on his lap and then pursing up her full lips to kiss him. "She did lots of work."

Her hot mouth closed on his, and the memories of her subtle flesh made his brain swirl. Lucy Hendricks was good. In the past, he'd usually gotten tired of a woman after a few weeks, but she had something. The expensive perfume he'd bought her in Yuma wafted up his nostrils. Then she began to tease his ears with her fingertips; he felt himself growing hard as she squirmed in his lap and her hot tongue sought his throat.

"Too early for that," he said, tearing his mouth away. "Besides, I hear horses coming. Get something on. They see you doing this to me, it'll make them boys so horny that I won't ever get any work out of them." He set her off his lap and on her feet. Then, with a playful slap on her rump, he sent her to the tent.

"All right," she said, looking back at him with her lids half closed. "But you know I'm ready when you are."

"I know that, honey."

He rose and stretched, glancing back as she disappeared. Grateful she was out of sight, he prepared himself for his men. He had business to take care of. Flannery and the boys were coming in.

His chief henchman, Mick Flannery, dismounted and handed his reins to Default, the small Frenchman who reminded Burns of a rat. The pimple-faced Kid sat the paint horse beside him. With his bowler hat and brown suit and vest, Flannery looked like a businessman as he strode up the hillside. He was nothing but an Irish thug—still, he did good work.

"How did it go?" Burns asked his man.

"McRoy's dead or he will be." Mick spat tobacco off to the side, then wiped his mustached mouth with the back of his hand.

"His claim?"

"No problem. I got Slow Tom McCleary up there sitting on it."

"Was it worth anything?"

"Some color, but I'm not sure," Flannery said with a shrug.

"Where did he get those nuggets we saw?" Burns looked hard at his man. What the hell had they killed McRoy for if his claim wasn't worth a damn?

"It probably came from digging," Flannery said to reassure him.

"Do we need to dig a shaft?" Burns asked, considering how a good strike would finance all his activities in Owl Creek. So far there had been no income, and it would soon deplete his wallet.

"Ain't anyone round to do it," Mick said. He frowned in disbelief at his boss's words. There wasn't a damn soul in the camp that he could hire. Slow Tom McCleary was a damn drunk, and only whiskey kept him sitting up there. The good ones, they were all working their own claims. He was lucky to have the hands he had.

"Then go to Prescott. Get some damn Chinks to dig it. And by the way, that Chinese girl didn't show up to work today. Lucy is pissed off as hell about it too."

"I'll get her back." Mick shook his head in defeat. What else would go wrong? That slant-eyed bitch needed a good thrashing, and then she'd learn her place.

"You better do that," Burns said. "I hate having that woman pissed." He glanced over at the tent to see if she was eavesdropping on them, then turned back to his henchman.

"I'll send Default to Prescott to get some Chinks to dig that shaft," Mick said. "How deep do you want to go?"

"How deep is the gold?" Burns scowled at the man. Damn, did he have to do all the thinking for this outfit?

"Damned if I know." Flannery removed his bowler for Lucy's sake as she swept out of the tent in a red silk duster that the wind wrapped around her legs. He felt himself getting hard at the very sight of her—damn, she must be angry about that bitch not showing up. "I'm going after that Chinese gal right now, ma'am," he said.

"I hope so," she said with her hands on her ample hips.

"Don't you worry your pretty head, little lady," he told her. "Mick does what he says he will do." Damn, all Burns had to do was climb on her ripe body and give orders to him. He drew in a deep breath as calmly as he could to control his anger. His heart raced—even when he was pissed off, she could shake him up.

Burns slipped his arm over her shoulder and hugged her possessively. He could see Mick almost drooling at her. Well, let him, that damn Frenchman, and Kid see who she belonged to. They could eat their damn hearts out wanting some of it. His hand slipped down until he cupped her butt;

she moved her hip against his, and then smiled up privately at him. His fingers squeezed her firm ass.

"Excuse me, ma'am?" Flannery made a little bow to her, and then walked down to speak to the Kid.

"You go down and find that slant-eyed bitch, get her ass up here, and don't be long doing it," Mick ordered. Then, for show, he slapped the Kid's paint on the rump to hurry him along. Satisfied the Kid would have her back in no time, he spoke to Default about going to Prescott. The Frenchman listened closely, and then nodded.

"What do I use for money?" he asked, looking in a quandary about what to do. "Why, I'll need to rent or buy a wagon to bring them back."

"He'll need money to hire them Chinks and a way to get them up here," Mick said aloud back to his boss.

"Here's fifty," Burns said with a look of displeasure as he drew it out.

Flannery gave it to Default. "Don't waste a dime of it. And don't come back without them Chinamen."

"I'll get them." Default waved to the two of them and then rode out.

Satisfied his man would do the job, Flannery walked back to Burns. "Got all that took care of, Boss. The Kid's gone to get Wee Woo or whatever the hell her name is, and Default's gone to Prescott to get them Chinamen to dig the shaft."

"Good, now you go by and check on that construction crew. The bunch down the street may beat us at this rate. I want to be the first saloon to open in Owl Creek. We're damn sure missing lots of gold dust right now by not having it open."

"Hell, they can't hatch it."

"Mick, I don't care what they do. I want it finished and open."

"We could get a big tent," Flannery suggested. Damn, he'd made that suggestion ten times.

"I don't want no damn carnival tent, I want a real saloon.

And another thing—buy us a team and wagon to haul things around in. We'll need it shortly for moving."

"I hear you. I'll see that it gets done. Good to see you, Miss Lucy." He tipped his hat again and went for his horse, which was grazing on the hillside.

"Nice to see you too," she said after him.

With all this money going out, Burns wanted some returns. He watched Flannery ride off. Maybe this McRoy mine would be the answer. That old man had known something that the rest didn't know when it came to gold mining. He'd bet that a shaft would find some real riches. In fact, he'd made a big gamble sending for the Chinks. For certain he needed a real gold mine to pay for those lazy carpenters and that plundering devil selling high-priced lumber down there. What was his name, Kramer?

Burns drew a deep breath of the pine-scented air. Soon this place would need a stage line to tie in with either Prescott or the Black Canyon stage. A man could make a fortune hauling out the rich ore and bringing in more folks. Besides, he would know the big shipments that were worth robbing. He'd better look into that soon before someone else had the same idea.

He stretched his arms over his head. Lucy moved in and pressed her body against his, then laid her cheek on his shirt.

"I'm ready for a room of our own," she said dreamily.

"Yeah, so am I, honey." He glanced over at the tent, considering the possibilities of them having some time alone. "That damn Kid'll be right back with Woo Wee, else I'd do something with you right now."

"I bet you would." She ran her hand over the hump in the front of his pants, then looked up at him as her fingers lingered. "Hmmm, my, my, it is a shame. That girl's name is Lou Wee."

"I don't care what her name is."

"Maybe you need some thin Chinese ass in your bed for a change."

"Hell, I can't keep *you* satisfied half the time. Why would I want more?" He knew exactly where she was trying to lead him. Women played the damnedest games. If he said he wanted to screw that bitch, then Lucy would be pissed off.

"She's young," Lucy said.

"She's ugly." What did he need to say next? He hated these games.

"I'm going to go inside and lie down," she announced in her dry husky voice.

"Good, I'm going to think about this mine deal." He needed no distractions. They had possession of the claim. He needed to try a quick shaft, maybe fifty feet deep, and then wash the diggings. That meant hauling the stuff to the creek and getting a claim there so he could use the water. That also meant he needed several ore wagons and teams to haul the ore. Who had those for sale?

Mick would know what kind and where to find them.

Burns dropped his butt in the chair and began to gaze across the countryside. The small clouds grew larger; soon they shaded some of the mountain peaks. Leaning back in the chair, he folded his arms over his chest and then crossed his outstretched legs. Lots to think about. The cool wind carried a hint of turpentine from the pines. Nice place to be, compared to the spiny desert south of there.

"You need help, missy?" the small Oriental girl asked, holding her hands together inside the worn blouse sleeves.

"Who are you?" Hap asked as she sat across from Slocum, ready to enjoy her first cup of coffee since the noon crowd had left the tables piled with dirty dishes and silverware.

"Me Lou Wee."

"You're new up here?" Hap turned her head to examine the girl.

"Yes. Come few days ago. Me wash dishes good."

"How much you charge me?"

"Feed me and two bits day. Me work cheap."

"Cheap enough. I'll try you. No funny business around my place. No Chinamen around here," Hap threatened her. "Them miners think I got a Chinaman cooking, they might quit eating my food."

"No, Chinaman." She shook her head and waved her small hands to impress Hap.

"Good. You had lunch?"

"No, but I clean up dishes first." The girl motioned to the tables.

"I'm real fussy. I use lots of soap and hot water on them."

"Me do it your way."

"The water is about hot. I'll be out there in a little while to show you how I want it. You can clear them and stack them back there for now."

"Plenty good." She bowed and hurried off in a shuffling gait to collect the metal dishes and crockery off the tables.

Hap studied her for a long moment as she worked. Then, as if satisfied, she turned back to Slocum and her coffee.

"Any kind of help will do." She shook her head to clear it.

"Looks to me like a blessing came down the road," Slocum said in approval.

"She could be. Them Orientals are real clannish. I wonder what she's doing up here all by herself. Ain't any others in camp I know about." She raised her brown eyebrows, and then shook her head in disappointment. Her hand shot out and patted his arm. "I'm a big help for you. I ask you to build a coffin and then someone steals your horse."

"Don't worry, I'll find another. I can borrow a cart from the carpenters next door," he offered. "And we can take the coffin out to the cemetery this evening after supper if you'd like."

"No need. The men will want to dig his grave. We won't have to. They like to put their own away. Most are thousands of miles away from their families, so they consider each other as family.''

"There you are, you damn dumb bitch!'' someone shouted out back of the tent.

They shared a frown. At the first shriek of the Chinese girl, Slocum jumped up and rushed out to see what was the matter. He came through the flap looking for her with his hand on his gun butt.

Some young cowboy had her by a thin arm and was dragging her off. Her feet were stuck in the ground, and he was having to physically haul her to get her to move. Slocum set out to separate them.

"Take your hands off her,'' Slocum said, and drove himself like a wedge between the two of them. The force of his drive made the pimple-faced boy drop his grip on her. His hand shot for his gun, but the muzzle of Slocum's .44 was already under his nose, cocked and ready, before he could even close his fingers on the rubber grip.

"Let go of that gun butt,'' Slocum said through his teeth.

"I did. I did.'' The Kid's spine straightened as he rose to his full height, looking cross-eyed at the barrel jammed harder into his face.

"What in the hell do you think you were doing with her?''

"Taking her back. She belongs to my boss.''

"There ain't no slaves left in this country.'' Slocum glared. "She obviously does not want to go with you to your boss or anyone else.''

"She hired on.''

"She quit.''

"I don't know who you are, but you ain't never messed with my boss.''

"What's his name?''

"Mick Flannery.''

"Tell him to come see me if he don't like it.''

"What's your name?''

"Slocum. What's yours?''

"The Val Verde Kid."

Obviously, Pimple Face had been reading too many dime novels for his own good. Slocum jerked the Colt from the Kid's holster, and then stepped back with it in his left hand. He holstered his own revolver, then stood squared off to the Kid, facing him. The girl had gone to the protection of Hap's arms. Both women eyed the Kid with some suspicion from the flap of the tent.

"You know his boss?" Slocum asked without turning away.

"Yes," Hap said.

"Kid, you better not mess around with her anymore. She don't work for your boss anymore. She works for Hap Arnold."

"You're going to regret this."

Slocum ignored his threat and punched the cartridges out of his revolver. They clinked on the ground. Then he handed the weapon back, butt first.

"Don't ever go for that thing again unless you have your coffin paid for."

"There will be another day, Slocum." After three unsuccessful tries, he had to look down to poke his empty gun in his holster.

"Pick that day well. It'll be your last," Slocum said, glaring hard at the pimple-faced Kid.

He watched him gather up his reins and then mount the paint. The Kid never looked back. Some punk that they slapped a name on—if he tried to live up to it, he would sure get himself planted before very long.

"You've made yourself a real enemy, Slocum," Hap said warily as she joined him. "That Mick Flannery is the cause of half the trouble in this camp. And the Kid works for him, all right."

"Then maybe we need to shut down that half of all the trouble in this camp." Every gold rush site had its own bullies until folks grew tired of them—some grew tired faster than others.

"I like your style, Slocum." Then, with the back side of her hand, she slapped him lightly on the chest. "You really don't give a damn, do you?"

"What good would it do?"

"None I can think of. Where did she go?" Hap searched around for the Chinese girl.

"Back inside to gather more dishes." He nodded in that direction, hearing the rattle of tin plates and dishes.

"Oh, good. Say, I've got to start supper or I'll never get it made in time."

"I'm going to look for a horse or a rig to drive."

"You're just going to run off?" she asked, looking at the ground.

"No, but since Stubben stole my horse and he ain't liable to come back with it soon, I'll need some transportation. I hate to walk."

"I was sort of wondering."

"You want something else?"

"Yes." She bobbed her head, then swept the hair back from her face. "I figured—well, maybe I could get you to build me that kitchen I need on the back of the tent. It don't have to be fancy. A roof and side walls. It would sure beat cooking outside in the rain is all."

"I'm not a carpenter." He narrowed his gaze at her. She didn't expect him to . . . yes, she did.

"You did fine on that coffin." She swept her hair back again. "You must have had some experience at it."

"Those two men next door did most of the work on it." He nodded in their direction.

"Yeah, I guess I'm asking too much."

"I'll think on it."

"Good." She smiled at his words. "You do that, Slocum. You sure think on that." Then she rushed off to help the girl clean up.

Markley, you rascal, you've got all my money and no doubt you are having a high old time on it somewhere between here and San Francisco. He headed around the tent. At the moment, he needed to find a horse to ride.

In deep thought, he paused to consider the contents of the fresh-board box by the tent wall. Who had shot that old man in the coffin? If Slocum only had his horse and gear back, he could go look around for some sort of evidence on who had killed him. What had started out as a simple search for his crooked ex-partner had turned into a full-time mess.

3

Slocum borrowed a saddle mule from Wiley. The lanky black jackass had never been well broken, and with the carpenter's saddle on him, he circled impatiently slobbering at the bits, as Slocum adjusted the stirrups down.

"I call him Bog," Wiley said from the unfinished back door of the saloon. "He does that often, bogs his head and bucks. He sure needs lots of riding."

Slocum nodded that he'd heard him while keeping his attention centered on the mule. If he could manage to ride the long-legged critter, he wanted to check out that old man's claim and see if he could learn anything there about his murder.

With the bridle cheek strap hard against his left leg, Slocum stepped up and into the saddle, and Bog began chasing his tail fast enough to make them spin. Slocum put both soles in the stirrups, then released his hold, and Bog let out the loudest bray, ducked his head between his knees, and bucked downhill for the road. Slocum sawed on his mouth, wishing for a spade bit instead of the snaffle in Bog's mouth.

Out of the corner of his eye he saw Hap on the rise,

shading her eyes with her hand and screaming for him to get off. Then the mule showed his best style and went high up, twisted, and then kicked in a final insult before he planted his four hooves on the hard road in a bone-jarring stop. Then he reared, and when he thought Slocum would kick free to keep from being fallen on, he leaped out into space.

Slocum saw his chance, and drove his spurs home. The shocked mule let out a high-pitched squall and dove off the road toward the creek.

Had he been a mustang, Slocum might have been ready to shake loose from the saddle, but he knew that a mule was not going to fall if he could help it. Bog's hooves hit the ground by the creek, and his hind feet came under him so fast he was forced to plunge into the water. Belly-deep in the stream and wide-eyed, he continued to try to buck, but his efforts were thwarted by the water.

Slocum pressed him on. At this point, Bog realized that his efforts were useless, and stopped and gave a final blow through the rollers in his nose. Slocum plow-reined him around toward the bank, and the mule obliged him. In two cat hops, he was on solid ground again. Once out of the creek, he shook like a dog, and then with his head down, went up onto the road like a broken animal.

"You all right?" Hap asked, skirt in her hand, hurrying down to Slocum as he halted the mule.

"Fine."

"There's folks would have gave ten bucks to seen that ride," Wylie said with his hat in his hand, looking impressed.

"I don't want to do it again," Slocum said, then laughed as the mule began to dance. "I better ride before he gets another notion." He waved to Hap and Wiley and set out.

"Be careful," she called after him.

He signaled that he had heard her, and set out in a long trot. The old man's claim was about three miles up the side canyon. From the directions various men had given him, he knew he was on the right track. He was looking for a log shack past a rock that looked like a standing Indian twice as tall as a man. A set of big elk horns was hailed over the door of the shack.

Lots of things needed answers. After he finished his investigation of the old man's claim, he planned to track down the horse thief. Either the thief had left the country and Slocum would never catch him, or he'd abandoned the horse not too far down the road, not wishing a necktie party for his efforts. Being a miner and not a cowboy, he'd probably left the dun somewhere close by. Slocum hoped that was the case.

The mule had a head-swinging gait, but Slocum had to kick him every so often to maintain it. The road narrowed to two rough tracks with short grass growing between them. It was not suited for wagons, making sharp turns over lots of rock outcroppings that would be rough to haul over.

He studied the good pine timber on the slope. It wouldn't be long until logging crews began to slash-harvest it for lumber and mine timbers. As he rode, he was grateful for the cool shade and the flitting birds that accompanied him. A striped ground squirrel stopped in the center of the track and looked at him curiously. Then, with a swish of his bushy tail, the sentry bolted away for the security of his burrow. His retreat drew a smile from Slocum as he pushed Bog onward and upward.

He reached the tall rock, and reined the mule up to let him breathe. Out of habit he checked his Colt, spinning the cylinder to see the loads. Satisfied, he holstered the weapon, studied the low-walled log structure up in the trees.

He could see the sun-bleached elk horns. There was no sign of smoke, but it was time for him to be cautious. If there were claim-jumpers, they could be dangerous. They'd killed once, and might kill again. He tried to see all he could, but the trees blocked his view. So he dismounted and loosened the girth, and Bog gave a snort in relief.

Best to tie him out of the way while he scouted the claim.

If someone was there, they would also be on guard. He took Bog up into the trees and tied him with a rope, not trusting the leather reins to hold him. With the mule out of sight and secure, he went downhill over the loose brown needles to circle the place and come in from the back side.

He crossed the road, still not seeing anyone. Cautiously, he slipped into the brush, and then he began working his way to the left of the shack. From his new position, he could make out a fresh pile of rock and dirt, obviously diggings, behind the cabin. His hand on his Colt, he reached the small stream and worked his way up to come behind the structure.

He made a quick check of the diggings. The old man had dug a pit almost twenty feet deep and fitted with a series of ladders to haul up his tailings. Slocum kept an eye on the shack as he knelt to examine what had been mined and piled. He used his left hand to examine the dirt. A dull familiar glint or two on his palm made him nod. Not rich ore, but it contained enough gold for a milling operation. The old man must have been close to something big here, and someone had figured it out and killed him for it.

Then too, his death might have been a simple "misunderstanding" between two men, with nothing at all to do with the claim. Miners could find the damnedest things to get mad at. Most disputes were settled with fists, but when the conclusion didn't suit one or both of them, guns, knives, even picks would settle the matter.

Cowboys fought over soiled doves and their personal dignity. Not miners. They fought because someone didn't like the Irish or British, or said something slurry about another's ancestors or mother. He'd seen two men fight with fists for two hours, and when it was over, fall on their butts exhausted. Often, battered to a pulp, blinded with swollen black eyes, neither could recall the source of their displeasure with each other in the first place.

Charlie McRoy had a good claim, so Slocum would stick with his first theory. He eased up to the side of the shack. Each log was well notched and sealed with adobe mud.

Painstakingly, Charlie had worked up the stream, washing his pan, getting more color, and all the time looking for the source. Satisfied with his find, he'd built the cabin with some pains and then begun his shaft. Damn shame that someone had ended his life. At the cabin's side, Slocum put his ear to the wall and heard a growl inside. He frowned at the sound.

Not a growl at all, he decided, but someone in there sleeping hard. He moved to the front door and lifted the latch string with his left hand, his right filled with the Colt. Using his boot sole, he kicked in the thick door and focused on the prone man in his underwear on the bed inside.

"Get your hands up!" Slocum shouted.

"Huh, what?" the whiskered man cried, jumping to his feet in panic.

Slocum crossed the room and shoved his Colt in the man's gut.

"You've got two seconds to tell me who killed Charlie McRoy."

"I don't know," the man replied. His eyes were wide open in fear, and he trembled so much, Slocum thought he might break apart. But Slocum had the advantage of surprise, and intended to use it to the fullest. If the man hadn't shot McRoy, he probably knew who had.

"Please, mister—I'm just watching this place for him."

"You work for Charlie?"

"Yeah, I work for Charlie. Gawd, put that gun away. I've got to go piss real bad. You scared the liver out of me." He shook his whiskered face in disbelief as he pushed his way outside.

Satisfied the man was unarmed, Slocum let him go and began to search the dark cabin. Only one bunk in the room. If this old man in his unwashed underwear worked for McRoy, where did he sleep? It wasn't adding up. He stepped to the door and looked for the man.

Where had he gone?

"Damn!" Slocum swore out loud as he ran around the

corner. That damned liar had run off barefoot and in his underwear. Chances were the old devil knew every nook and cranny in the canyon and could easily hide from him. Slocum stood under the pines listening to the racy scolding of a magpie—*got careless and lost him, didn't you?*

Up on the mountainside, Bog brayed as if he too knew about the man running off. It would be hard to run him down wherever he went. Besides, the day was almost gone. Slocum had better get back to camp—nothing more he could do there. With a deep sigh of disgust, he went after his mule.

On foot, Flannery hurried up the hill in the late afternoon. More men were coming into the camp all the time, hiking in, on wagons and carts, even on burros. He wanted to open a tent saloon and pick them clean. But Harvey Burns hated tent saloons and wouldn't hear of it. Well, if he had one up now, he'd have all the gold dust in camp. They needed to do something before that Prescott bunch got their saloon finished down by the woman's tent.

He shook his head as he climbed the steep portion. He couldn't get enough work out of Burns's crew. They were laggards, and any threat on his part fell on deaf ears. Maybe he ought to lay his knife on someone's throat while they slept, wake them all, and tell them that if they didn't get to working they'd have their jugulars cut. But they'd probably quit and run away first chance they got. That would sure make Burns mad.

He better go check on that old drunk up at the shack. Counting on drunks for anything was risky business. If pressured, that old man might spill his guts.

Then there was the incident with the Kid earlier down at that woman's tent. Some cowboy had backed the kid off, taking that Chinese bitch away. Lucy would be pissed about that. Who in the hell was he? There was no end to Flannery's troubles. Maybe the Prescott bunch building the other saloon had hired the cowboy.

He had to learn more about them. Jesus, there was a lot for him to do. He stopped to catch his breath. His heart pounded hard, giving him a headache as he paused to rest and view the camp. A cool north wind swept his face. It was going to be cold when the sun set. He studied the bank of clouds; it might even rain. With his breath back, he hurried on to Burns's tent. He could see the two of them seated at the table outside, eating their evening meal like a king and queen.

"What's going on?" Burns asked, looking up from his supper. "I haven't seen that China bitch you promised Lucy."

"Some gunhand stopped the Kid when he went after her. Seems she's working for that Arnold woman." He almost shuddered, expecting an angry tirade from Burns.

"Who in the hell does he work for?" Burns shared a disgusted frown with Lucy, who sat across the table from him. He continued to eat as if Flannery wasn't standing there.

"Maybe he works for that Prescott bunch building the other saloon," Flannery said.

"We need to find out who they are." Burns never looked up, acting busy slicing his meat and grumbling to Lucy that it was tough.

"It came tough," she said under her breath.

"Yeah well, you didn't help it any," Burns said.

"Yeah, well, you two promised me help and I haven't seen her yet," Lucy said.

"I'll get her myself," Flannery finally promised.

"Do that, and find out who this gunhand is who interfered and who he works for." Burns stabbed the air with his fork in Flannery's direction.

"No one knows him. He's a stranger, but I'll find out."

"Flannery, things aren't going like I like for them to go down there."

"I can't do everything alone. The Kid, hell, he's a kid. And Default is gone to get your diggers."

Burns deliberately wiped his mouth on the linen napkin. Then, taking his time, he cleaned his hands on it. Flannery dreaded every small move he made. No doubt, Burns was upset at the turn of events.

"Get it straightened out!" Burns finally roared, then lowered his voice. "Did you find a wagon and team yet?"

"Not yet. Some guy in camp has one. I'll see him in a little bit about them."

"We'll need one. Good. But find out who this gunhand works for that's giving you trouble."

"I will. Good night." Flannery turned on his heel, anxious to be away from Burns; he expected to be showered with more of his boss's rage before he was out of range of his voice.

"No more mistakes!" Burns called after him.

Flannery hurried down the hill in the growing twilight. Thunder growled in the distance and made him frown; rain was coming. He'd do something about this Slocum fella in the morning. He half ran to go find the man who had the team for sale. He would have to check around—he had forgotten the man's name.

Slocum had ridden into camp, put the mule out on a long rope, and carried Wiley's saddle and gear up to the unfinished saloon. He slung it on the floor, grateful for its use. But no one was there to thank, so he hurried for Hap's tent.

Inside, supper was being served. He waved to her as she worked, and then began to talk with some of the miners about a riding animal for sale. No one knew of a good saddle horse, but he did learn there was a team and wagon for sale.

He left the tent as she stirred about serving the many customers. There were lots of unasked questions on her face as he waved good-bye. He hurried on foot to find the man who had the outfit for sale.

He found him and his rig on the other side of the camp. Slocum stood for a long while and studied the light team and wagon. The two blacks needed some feed, but they were sound, strong enough to pull a load. He could haul the materials for her kitchen in from Prescott at a big savings—if he could buy the team at the right price.

"Fifty dollars is my last offer," Slocum said. "I wouldn't even consider them, but that shooter Stubben stole my saddle horse."

"Ain't enough money. Why, the harness is worth that much," the man complained.

"Take it or leave it."

The man shook his head in disappointment. "Guess I've got to take it. Need enough grub to get me through digging a shaft on my claim."

"Ain't many folks needing horses up here, I guess," Slocum said, comfortable with his purchase as he counted out the money to the man.

" 'Cause no one's leaving. There is just enough color to make you think any minute you'll hit the big mother lode, and only a fool would leave good color."

"Hey, farmer!" a short man with hard features shouted as he came hurrying down the road. "I want to buy that team of yours."

"You're too late, Flannery, Slocum just bought them." The man shoved the roll of money down in his pants pocket.

"Slocum! You're the one that pistol-whipped the Kid?" The man made a move to sweep his coattail back and expose his gun.

"I'm the man who stopped him. But you better be damn sure what you're doing with that gun there." Slocum said.

"I know what I'm doing." Flannery's hand was poised inches away from the grips. He flexed his fingers as if itching to go for it.

"You kill an innocent bystander here, folks might want to stretch you neck."

"They ain't getting mine, mister."

"Besides, if I'd pistol-whipped that Kid, he wouldn't

have been able to got back to you by now."

"You were meddling in my business."

"No, Flannery, he was messing where he didn't belong.
Now put your hand down. Only a fool or a drunk would
buck someone he hasn't ever seen draw before."

"You saying you're fast?" Flannery squinted his eyes
at him.

"No, but I'm sure."

"What the hell does that mean?" Flannery folded his
arms over his chest defiantly.

"Means I've lived this long, so I must be faster than
most."

"What's your game here anyway? I'll give you a twenty-
dollar profit on that team."

"Generous enough, but I've got some hauling to do. I
may sell them in a month."

"I won't need them in a month."

"I guess they sell horses all over this world. Thank you,
sir," Slocum said to the miner, who'd stepped back. Ignoring Flannery, Slocum climbed on the seat.

Then he glanced for a last time at the Irishman. The
man's mouth was drawn in a thin line; he looked ready to
burst, standing there with his chin squeezed in the fingers
of his left hand.

"I don't know who the hell you are, Slocum, but by
gawd, I'll remember you." With that, Flannery turned on
his heel and marched up the street.

"That ain't good," the man who sold him the team said
with a look of concern on his face.

"Hell, he don't know how many people remember me
now." They both shared a grin. Slocum clucked to his team
and turned them around in the road. They were gentle
enough, and with some grain and care they'd be able to
tote a load.

How many trips from Prescott would it require to get the
lumber up there for Hap's kitchen? No telling. Slocum lit
a cigar as he drove them toward her tent. He drew in

deeply and considered his next move. He'd met Flannery and was not impressed with what he had seen. There were hundreds of his kind in the West—and they bore close watching.

He'd been on the go hard for two weeks looking for his ex-partner, to no avail. Might as well stay up here. Markley would probably spend the money before Slocum ever found him. Besides, Slocum had taken sort of a fancy to this Hap woman, and for certain she needed some help getting her place started.

Back at her place, he took off the harness and stored it under a canvas sheet. The wall of rain coming down the valley made him hurry in the gathering darkness. With his new team staked out in good grass for the night, he hurried for the lamp glow under the canvas.

In the empty tent, she looked up from her place at a center table. A smile of relief spread over her face at the sight of him. Thunder drummed harder down the valley.

"I found a team and bought them," he announced.

"Good. Did they cost much?"

"No, I made a real bargain. I can get my money out of them anywhere."

"Sounds wonderful—the horses, I mean. I saved you some food," she said, getting up to go after it.

"I could stand some food." He took a place on the bench across from where she had been sitting.

"What did you find up there today at Charlie's claim?" she asked over her shoulder.

"Some old drunk sleeping in the shack. He stank of bad whiskey, and there were enough empty bottles laying around for two drunks."

"What did he look like?" She returned and put the heaping plate before him.

"Skinny, about five-nine, gray whiskers, dirty as a rat."

"That's Slow Tom. He's worthless. He sure didn't shoot Charlie, did he?" She folded her skirt under her, then sat down beside him with her back to the table.

"No, but he might have been guarding the claim for someone else."

"Like Flannery?" she asked.

"Yeah. I met him. But I don't have a thing to link them. Do you?"

"No."

He began to eat the food. He savored it as they exchanged notions about why Flannery had tried to buy the team and his possible involvement in McRoy's death. She reminded him that the Kid worked for him or did his bidding, and so did a rat-faced Frenchman named Default. They would all bear watching, he decided as he finished eating. He slid the empty plate toward her, and then rose to go check on the rain at the tent flap.

"Where do you plan to sleep tonight?" she asked from behind him as he stood and watched the sheets of rain in the dim twilight. "I just figured out that the horse thief took your bedroll too," she added.

"He got my slicker too," he said with a half smile as he turned to face her.

"I don't have one of those to fit you, but I can loan you some blankets and you can sleep in here. I've got a small tent out back for a little privacy." She motioned toward it with her head. Then she set her hair back from her face.

"Seeing as the Grand Hotel isn't open . . ." They both laughed out loud. Then, in the flickering light of the hanging coal oil lamp, Slocum saw a flush of embarrassment cross her face.

"Guess I'm kinda forward," she said with a shrug, and avoided looking at him.

"Don't worry about that. I'll be going to Prescott at first light for the first load of lumber. Maybe up there I can find out something about my stolen horse too. At the least I can report the thief to the sheriff."

"How much money will you need for the materials?"

"I doubt I can get over fifty dollars worth of lumber on a farm wagon and get it back up here."

"Kramer ain't going to like the competition." She looked at him for an answer with her lips pursed together.

"No one likes competition in this town." He met her gaze.

"I was just saying."

"Sorry. It's been a tough day for both of us."

"You're excused." She drew a roll of bills from her apron pocket and counted the money out for him.

"You don't even know me. I could keep going with this," he said in disapproval.

"I doubt it." She wrinkled her nose. "I figure that I can trust you."

"They put off burying the dead man until sunup?" he asked, seeing the coffin in the corner of the tent.

"Yeah, this downpour coming in had them worried." Thunder punctuated her words. She closed down the flaps and tied the strings to keep out the wind. Her shadow from the coal oil lamp danced on the tent sides.

Slocum sat down on a bench at the table. He could see the weariness in her face. Feeding this many miners was no small project. How long the flighty Chinese girl would stay and work for her was anyone's guess. Hap needed more help, but that was impossible to find for the moment. One thing about her, and he admired her for it, she was a fighter.

She gave a great sigh and sat down beside him.

"Where have you been all my life, Slocum? You must have other things to do in your life besides haul my lumber up here and mess with my building."

"Nope. I've given up on a claim in the Dragoons. Not enough silver. While I was working it, my ex-partner sold our saloon over in Silver City and ran off with the proceeds, and I figure he's lost it all in a poker game by now anyway. So why not spend a cool summer up here in the Bradshaws and build you a start on your cafe."

She turned and threw her arms around his neck. Without a pause, she kissed him hard on the mouth. He met her lips with his own. Her firm breasts furrowed into his chest. With his eyes closed, he savored the sweetness and the need she transmitted to him. At last, out of breath, they gasped for air, cheek to cheek in each other's arms, and slowly recovered as the cool air invaded the tent and caused her to shudder.

"You cold?" he asked.

"Maybe more scared than anything else." She squirmed to get closer against him.

"No need to be afraid."

"I know. I just never get involved like this with the men in my life."

"Time for a change," he said in her ear.

"Yes," she agreed, and then she sought his mouth again.

At last, she twisted her face from his. With a newfound resolve, she slipped from his arms, pushed them aside like a tempted child refusing a bribe, then scooted a short distance away on the bench.

"I feel cheap, like I'm bribing you to do this," she told him.

"I bribe cheap," he said with a smile.

"I can pay you for your work and that hauling." She looked at her hands in her lap as if inspecting them.

He stood up, lifted the glass chimney, and then blew out the lamp. Darkness engulfed the tent.

"Who says I'm looking for money?" he asked.

"Are you serious?" she asked, forcing down a laugh.

"Dead serious." He stood up, taking her by the arm. She rose to meet him. His hands cupped her firm butt, pulling her hard against him. As their need for each other soared, he began to raise her skirt until his fingers could clutch the satin skin of her thighs. She gasped at his touch, and locked her arms around his neck.

"Oh, gawd, I wasn't going to let this happen—" She reached down and helped him hoist the dress up to her waist. Then, in the dim light of the tent, she winked, quickly unbuttoned her bloomers, and shoved them off her hips in haste.

"Where do you want me?" she asked breathlessly, stepping out of them.

"On the table."

"Yes," she whispered in a husky voice. "I serve everything else there." Her excited laughter made him want to hurry as she stood on her toes and then hoisted herself on the tabletop. He fumbled at the gunbelt buckle, undoing it. Out of breath and about to shake with his need for her, he laid the holster on the bench. She worked her dress out from under her butt, exposing her shapely white thighs in the faint light as she situated herself on the edge of the table.

His pants down to his knees, he unleashed his turgid root from his underwear and scooted up until he stood between her legs. His breath raged through his nose as she eased herself down on her back. The feel of her firm legs around his waist made him shiver. With his throbbing manhood in his fist, he pointed it into her gates. The way parted for his entry, and she gave a small cry. His hips ached to surge deeper inside her, and slowly he began to thrust himself into her as she made small sounds of pleasure.

He planned to savor her as he held her legs in the crooks of his arms. His luck wasn't all bad. He'd lost his horse, bedroll, razor, a few other personal things—but what the hell! His palms ran over her firm butt, and he began to seek her depths with all his might. The waves of contractions inside her began to thicken. Their breathing reached a rage as they tried to draw the most from each other. His shaft reached its full proportion, and filled her like an oversized lead bullet rammed into a muzzle-loader.

Then she cried out loud and raised herself up for his deepest probe. At last, with a loud moan, she collapsed on the table. He held her legs up as he fought to end his own agony. Then, as he strained with each plunge, relief rose like a volcanic explosion, and ended in a fiery blast that caused him to slam hard into her.

Fighting for his breath, he released her legs and slipped out of her. With some effort, and his help, she sat up as if drunk. Then she put her hands on his shoulders for support; they both gasped for air.

"Oh, gawd, Slocum, where have you been?" she managed at last.

"I've been coming," he said as he lowered his mouth to kiss her. His legs felt about to collapse under him as he spread his hands on the tabletop on each side of her to move in to savor her sweetness. More thunder peeled off in the distance.

"Come sleep in my tent with me?" she managed.

"It may ruin your reputation."

"Reputation—hell—" she said. Then, without impulse, she kissed him wetly and cupped his neck in her hand to keep him close to her face.

He listened to the light rain on the canvas. Fate had brought him here—why not? "Sure."

"I may not let you sleep," she teased.

"You may play hell keeping me up," he said. Using his hands to clutch her waist, he helped her off the table. She pulled her skirt down, and bent over and retrieved her bloomers in the dim light. He steadied her when she stood up with her prize.

"I better not leave them there," she teased.

"Better not."

She clung to his waist as they staggered down the aisle between the tables to the rear of the tent. "I may just keep you awake," she said.

They both laughed at her threat.

Flannery had gone back to seek his boss's advice about Slocum and how to handle him. Instead he met Burns's instant ire, and knew he had done the wrong thing to even go up there again.

"Who is this bastard? First, he whips up on the Kid! Then he buys that team out from under you!" Burns surged out of the chair. Rain drummed on the roof of the tent and thunder rolled down the valley as Burns glared in anger at Mick.

"Some Texas hardcase," Flannery told his boss as the big man dropped his frame back down in the seat.

"What does that mean?" Burns frowned.

"He's a gunhand."

"One damn Texan and you and the Kid want to go hide?"

"I've seen his kind before."

"Get rid of him. What's the matter, Mick, lost your nerve?"

"I'll get him!" Flannery rose without another word. He ducked, going out the flap, and stomped off in the rain, pissed as hell that his boss had not even offered a hand. Damn, Burns would stay up there in his dry tent with that sweet Lucy and let Flannery do all the damn dirty work.

First thing, he had to lay a good trap for Slocum. To do that, he had to know where he stayed and his habits. Then they'd eliminate him. That Texas gunhand would turn up one morning facedown in a mud hole.

The cool mist swept Flannery's face as he hurried downhill in the inky night. That lazy bunch building the saloon had probably quit early with this rain.

Lightning blinded him. The crash shook him as his soles slipped in the slick mud underfoot, but he grasped for a bough and saved himself from falling down. Damn rain anyway. The wetness soaked through to his shoulders as he reached the road and hurried up it for the small shack that served as his headquarters and the place where the nails and tools were stored each night by the crew.

He pushed inside the shack's door as another gravedigger creased the entire sky and illuminated the tent city. They needed a tent saloon set up and doing business, as slow as those carpenters were getting along. Their competitors would have theirs up and finished in no time. This next week the push would be on. Once the roof was on the other one—he tried to strike a match. The damp head crumbled without lighting. He dug out another as his temper flared. The fifth one snapped alive, and he lit the candle lamp.

He'd put up with a lot to make it this far. He'd been born in New York City, and his mother had worked as a washerwoman and sometime whore when she could find a man who wanted her body. Since he'd been ten years old, he'd been on his own, at first stealing things to eat and survive. Then later, in St. Louis, he'd met Danny O'Grady. Danny Boy had taught him all about skull-knocking and how to eliminate anyone who got in his way. At sixteen, by himself, he'd slipped his first victim into the Mississippi. A trapper he'd killed for his purse, rifle, and horse.

Things had gotten too thick for him in St. Louis after that, and he'd headed west. He'd worked as a bouncer at "hog ranch" outside Fort Russell. One night he'd beaten too hard on a drunk soldier raising hell with one of the whores, and had left there under the cover of night.

He was working as a faro dealer and bartender in the Lady Luck Saloon in Yuma when Harvey Burns arrived by a Colorado River paddle wheeler from the Gulf of California. They hit it off, and soon were headed with Default and the Kid for Prescott. Burns claimed all they needed was the right setup, and the word on the Owl Creek rush arrived a week after they got to Prescott.

Where was the Kid? Not in his bunk. That punk was no hardcase, that was for sure. He was probably sniffing around that whore who'd come in with that gambler a few days earlier. Meanwhile, Flannery still needed to find a wagon and team. Burns wanted them for some damn reason. If that Default didn't succeed in getting those Chinks hired, Flannery's ass would be in bigger trouble with Burns.

He looked out the small window in the direction of his boss's camp. The candle's light flickered on the stacked barrels of beer. Why Burns didn't let him throw up a saloon tent, he'd never know. His stubborn decision was damn sure costing him gold dust. Those miners were looking for places to spend their finds.

He removed his coat and hung it to dry on the chair back. The rain was about over as night settled in the valley. He poured himself a glass of whiskey. The liquor cut the phlegm in his throat. Nothing ever was easy. He'd first thought they would easily get control over the camp, but each day the task grew harder and harder to handle.

This damn Slocum was another thing in their road. Flannery poured himself a second glass of whiskey. What made this fella the protector of that Arnold woman? He considered her full figure as he held up the glass of amber liquor—he'd like to stick his cock in her too. With a new resolve, he tossed down the whole glass. He'd sleep a couple of hours. Maybe then he could figure out what to do about Slocum. He began to feel the whiskey—it would let him rest. He never slept over a few hours at a time anyway, even drunk. He stripped down to his underwear and then fell across the lower bunk. His eyes closed and he drew in a deep breath, surrendering to sleep.

Someone stumbled into the shack. He awoke, sat up, and grasped the revolver in his hand, trying to make out who had come inside.

"Kid, that you?" He heard whoever was there in the darkness coughing and shivering. No answer.

"Gawdammit, who's there?"

"Me," the voice gasped.

"That you, Slow Tom?" He frowned. What was Tom doing down there? He was supposed to be up at McRoy's cabin. What had gone wrong? Damned old drunk anyway . . .

"Yeah. It's me, Mick."

"Why ain't you at the claim?"

"Jesus, I'm freezing to death." Tom pulled a blanket from the Kid's bunk and wrapped himself up in it. His teeth chattered like dinner plates on a rocking train.

What in the hell had happened? What was that old son of bitch doing out in the damn cold rain anyway? Flannery's bare feet hit the floor. He crossed the room and shut the door before someone passed by and learned what was going on. Then he lit the lamp again.

"Some guy in a cowboy hat come—asked a lot of questions," Tom said. "I ran away from him."

"In your underwear, for Christ sake?"

"I had no damn choice. You got anything to drink in here?"

"Yeah." Flannery studied the old man shaking under the blanket, showing dark spots of wetness on his narrow shoulders. His thin hair was matted down on his small peaked head.

"Yeah," Flannery repeated. "I've got some whiskey. You need some bad, don't you?"

"Yeah, I had some hard times coming down here. I got the shakes bad. Had to stop couple of times, that's why I didn't beat the rain. Oh, gawd, I'm cold." He trembled visibly.

Flannery poured him some whiskey in a glass. The rain drummed down. First off, Flannery needed to know what this old drunk had told this cowboy. *Must be Slocum.* Nothing—nothing ever went as Flannery planned. If the old bastard had been on his guard, a few stray shots and that damn Slocum would have left unsuspecting. The problem now was how much Slocum had found out from Tom.

"Here. What did you tell him, Slow Tom?"

"Nothing." His white hands shook hard as he reached for the drink. Flannery grasped his wrist to hold him back for a minute.

"You want that drink bad?"

"Yeah, I sure do," Tom's strained voice said in a hoarse whisper.

"Then you tell me what you told him!"

"Nothing, Mick, I swear. On my mother's grave, I

swear, Mick, nothing. I run off and been walking barefoot to get here and warn you."

"Warn me of what?"

"That he come up there poking around."

"A cowboy, huh?"

"Yeah, wore a big hat, a hardcase, Mick."

"I know who you mean. Drink the damn whiskey." He looked away at the shadows on the wall. It was Slocum, all right—only one man in camp matched that description and would be poking his nose in other people's business. Flannery had another problem besides Slocum. The old man had outlived his usefulness. Time to end his misery. Let him drink the whiskey—everyone deserved one last round.

"What you want me to do?" the old man asked between deep gulps. "I got to have some clothes. Can't go anywhere in my underwear."

"I'll take care of that."

"I knew you would, Mick. That's why I came straight here. You know I wouldn't talk, Mick, you know that."

"Sure." With that, Flannery struck him over the head with his pistol butt, and he fell facedown on the floor.

The door swung open to the night and a startled Kid stood in the doorway, staring at the prostrate body on the floor.

"What the hell's going on?" he demanded.

"Get in here and shut the damn door," Flannery ordered. "We've got work to do."

"Who's that?"

"Slow Tom. That cowboy that stopped you from getting that girl, he jumped Tom up at the claim. Asked the old man lots of questions, but Tom ran off from him. We need to get rid of Tom and quick so he don't talk. You can't trust an old drunk."

"What—what we going to do with him?" The Kid stood with his back to the closed door as if he wanted lots of distance between him and the old man sprawled on the floor.

"Get hold of his legs," Flannery ordered as he began to dress.

"Huh?"

"Pick up his legs! We've got to haul him to the creek and drown him."

"What?"

"So it looks like an accident. Get his legs."

"Gawdamn, it's pissing and pouring out there." Another bolt of lightning shook the small glass window. "We'll get killed."

"You grab his legs or I'll shoot your ass right here and now." Dressed and with his shoes on, Flannery straightened and narrowed his eyes at the Kid. He'd had all the lip he intended to take from that punk.

"All right, but we get hit by lightning, it'll be all your fault."

Flannery put on his oilskin coat and then took the old man's arms. With the body between them, he and the Kid shuffled outside into the downpour.

A blinding bolt struck on the hillside and illuminated the rain-drenched valley as they struggled to carry the limp load toward the creek. The old man began to moan as the cold downpour revived him.

"He's waking up," the Kid said between grunts.

"Shut up, I can hear him."

"What are we going to do?"

"Shut up," Flannery said, so mad he could drown the Kid too. His feet slipped in the mud, then he recovered. They were only fifty yards from their destination. So far, so good—no one had seen them.

"Mick—where you—taking me?" the old man managed.

"The doctor."

"I don't need a doctor, Mick. I'm freezing. Jesus, I'm cold. Where you going with me—Mick?"

"Shut up!" the Kid said, straining as they half fell going down the steep bank with their burden.

"Mick, I never told him a thing." Tom's voice raised to a high desperate pitch. "You got to believe me. I never—"

"You never will either!" Flannery said as they dumped him into the stream. Then Flannery gritted his teeth, gripped Tom's thin shoulders in his fingers, and plunged the man's head underwater. Slow Tom made a feeble attempt to reach up and stop him. But he was desperate for breath, and at last began to gulp in water as Flannery stood knee deep, submerging him with all the force in his arms and body.

And you won't ever tell a soul. Die, you old bastard, die!

4

Dawn came with the smoke of her cooking fires; Slocum
already had the horses hitched and ready to go. The cool
freshness of the pine-scented morning filled the quiet valley. He was ready to leave for Prescott as she rang the
triangle for breakfast. Then he stepped up in the wagon
box. She tossed him the roll of blankets that she'd fixed
for him to sleep in and the sack of food she'd prepared for
him to take along.

"You be careful," she said, and stepped up on the wheel.
"How long will it take?"

"I'll be back in a couple days," he said. Then he leaned
over and stole a quick kiss from her as the sleepy miners
began to appear in the long shadows. She licked her lips,
looked ready to say something, and instead stepped down,
took her skirt in hand, and ran off to join Lou Wee at the
serving table.

Slocum untied the reins and clucked to the team. He
waved to her and then swung them around. It was a long
ways to Prescott, maybe forty miles. The worst part would
be the grades. One thing for certain, the road would be
crude all the way there.

By mid-morning he had reached the first flat stretch since he'd started out of the deep canyon. He stopped to allow the horses to breathe. They had done good, but the wagon was empty. A noisy jay in a high pine bough scolded him. He grinned at the saucy bird and then, ready to go on, undid the lines and clucked to the team.

At noon he arrived in Iron Mountain, another scruffy mining camp of clapboard buildings and tent structures lined up on a dry rutted street. He smiled when some curs ran out to challenge him. This place had been there long enough to have its own town dogs. Forced to drive around some freight wagons, he kept his eye out for any sight of his dun horse. There was no telling how far the thief had gone.

"Hey!" a gal in a thin petticoat shouted at him from the log porch of a saloon. "Is that you, Slocum?"

He glanced around to see if anyone had heard her. He never knew who might be listening. She stood in a thin shift that left nothing to his imagination—even her navel showed through the silky material.

"Yeah, Mae, it's me," he said, recognizing her, and reined in the team, grateful to see the familiar soiled dove again. Where had he seen her last? Tombstone? He couldn't recall.

Short and shapely, she hurried off the crude porch to meet him. He tied off the lines and jumped down. When they met, he swept her off her feet in his arms and swung her in a circle. She kissed him on the mouth.

He set her down, and then she tugged the short hem down on her shift to cover her shapely behind as her blue eyes glistened.

"What are doing with that outfit?" she asked, motioning to his wagon.

"A thief stole my dun horse. His name is Stubben. You seen a big dun horse? This Stubben's got black whiskers, wore a plaid shirt and canvas pants. Had lots of black hair."

"He was through here last night, I think. I wondered

where a miner got a cowboy outfit, Texas saddle and all.''

"He rode on?"

"Yeah. I haven't seen him today. You up at that new strike on Owl Creek?"

"Yes."

"Any color up there?"

"Some. They're working like beavers looking for more."

"I might ought to head over there. There must be a whore for every miner here that's got any gold." She looked at the sky for help.

"Business should be wide open up there."

"Ain't what I heard." She gave him a wry scowl. "That damn Irishman up there is getting his take from everybody."

"Everybody?"

"Yes. That Mick Flannery was down here couple of weeks ago. Told a bunch of us girls if we came up that he'd let us work for fifty-fifty. You can't make enough on your back to pay him that much."

"I'll be back in few days with a load of lumber. I'll look after you if you want to go up there."

"You're a good man," she said with a grin, standing on her toes and kissing him on the cheek. Then she pulled the shift back down over her shapely butt. "You've got a deal."

"Did you see which way that miner went with my dun?" he asked, considering the horse thief again.

"Prescott, I guess," she said with a shrug.

"Thanks. See you in a few days. Oh, you better get yourself a tent to use up there. There aren't any buildings finished yet." He undid the leather reins and kicked off the brake.

"I will." She waved at him as she climbed on the porch, exposing most of her shapely behind from under the short shift. Then, with a mischievous wink at him, she deliberately pulled the hem down again.

He clucked to the horses as they started up a grade. Thunderheads were building. There would be showers in the Bradshaws somewhere that afternoon. And he didn't have a slicker.

5

Long past dark, he came off the mountain with his jaded horses into Prescott. The sleeping town was scattered over the hills. A dim lamp shone on the sign hanging out in front of Pense's livery. He had covered lots of ground, missing several showers that had swept up another mountain beside his. He reined up in front of the wagon yard, both horses giving a loud snort. Then they dropped their heads.

"Can I help you, mister?" a boy in his mid-teens asked.

"How much to put up my horses, water, grain them, and rub them down?" He climbed off the seat and tried his legs. He bent over to stretch them. Man, driving a wagon that far was sure hard on him. Every muscle in his body ached.

"Fifty cents?" the boy asked cautiously.

"You have a deal." Slocum straightened, dug out the money, and handed the boy the coins. "Has a man rode in here on a big stout dun horse sometime today? Texas saddle. The dun's a big horse close to sixteen hands. Got a CK brand. This man is a miner—no hat, beard, black hair."

"That horse is inside, mister," the kid said, looking up strangely at him.

51

"Good," Slocum said, looking around. "Where's the fella who rode in on him?"

"I reckon he's over there on Whiskey Row across from the courthouse."

"Where's the sheriff?" Slocum looked around to get his bearings.

"Asleep this time of the night, I'd say."

"Good place to be," he agreed, listening to the distant sound of tinny pianos and the peal of some soiled dove's laughter that shattered the darkness. "That where all the saloons are at?"

"Sure are. All of them are right there across the street from the jail. A whole block of them. Saves the law hauling them far when they need jailin'."

"I see. Thanks."

"You going over there and pick a fight with the man stole your horse?"

"No, I'm going to try to find the law and get them to arrest him."

"You need to see Marshal Cribbs at the courthouse. He's on duty—he'll bring him in for you."

"How's my dun?" Slocum tossed his head back toward the dark stables.

"Tired when he rode him in, but he's a stout horse. He's in a tie stall about halfway back." The boy held up his lantern. "I'll show you."

"Good. I'll check on him and be sure that he's mine. Then I'll go find this Marshal Cribbs."

"I'll take good care of your team too while you're doing that, mister."

"I'm counting on it," Slocum said, following the youth back into the barn with the deep aroma of sour horse manure hanging heavy in the air.

The dun nickered to him when he spoke. His horse looked none the worse. The big CK brand was on his hip. Slocum bent down and ran his hands over the pony's legs for splints, and then decided Stubben hadn't hurt him.

"He leave my saddle, rifle, bedroll, and things?"

"Yeah, they're up front on the rack in the office."

"Good." The next thing he had to do was find that marshal.

"Funny thing," the kid said.

"What's that?"

"He never acted like no horse thief. We had them come in before, but they acted edgy like the law's breathing down their neck. He never did."

"Take my word for it, he was one."

"Oh, I do, sir."

In the courthouse on the second floor, Slocum located the portly marshal with his dusty boots propped up on the open middle drawer of his desk. Dressed in a black frock coat and a small string tie, the man puffed on a thick cigar, and a blue haze filled the room.

"What be your business?" the man asked, taking the stogie from his mouth to speak.

"Come to claim my horse that a man stole and to get you to arrest him."

"Serious business, accusing a man of horse stealing." He put his boots down. Then he took up a pen and paper. "Let's get it all down. You find the horse?"

"It's over at the wagon yards."

"Good. Who took it?"

"His name is Stubben, they say."

"Who's they?" The lawman cocked his head sideways and looked at Slocum perturbed.

"Miners up on Owl Creek. This Stubben shot an unarmed man in cold blood yesterday, and then he stole my horse to get away on."

"That's murder too." The lawman narrowed his bushy brows closer as if testing the honesty of Slocum's charge.

"Yes, he's guilty of that too."

"Murder, horse thieving, what else we going to charge him with?" Cribbs held his pen ready.

"I don't care. He took my bedroll, slicker, rifle, saddle, and gear when he took the horse."

"Worth more than twenty bucks?"

"I'd say so."

"Murder, grand larceny, and horse stealing. Where is this Stubben at?"

"The boy at the stables thought that he was across the street in one of them saloons. He's been in town a while, I'd say."

"Highly likely." The lawman scratched a bushy eyebrow as if considering the matter, and then with effort rose to his feet. He removed a sawed-off double-barrel from the rack of weapons on the wall, and motioned for Slocum to go ahead.

"I'm coming right after you." He paused to slap on a wide-brim black hat.

They crossed the street and ducked around a freight wagon, and the lawman motioned toward the center saloon in the block. Cribbs went through the swinging door, holding the scattergun to his chest, and a silence fell over the crowd. Every eye followed him as he crossed to the bar. Slocum took a place in the shadows with his back to the wall beside the door. And waited.

"We're looking for a miner—name of Stubben," Cribbs announced to the bartender.

"Hell, I don't know no Stubben. Do you, Harry?" he asked the other barkeep.

"Don't know him," the second man said.

"New man in town, big, with black hair, a miner," Cribbs said again, the ring of impatience edging in his deep voice.

"Anyone in here know a Stubben?" the first bartender asked out loud. The room's hush was deep enough to hear a pin drop.

Cribbs seemed satisfied that Stubben wasn't in there, and came back across the room, ready to go check another saloon. Their man wasn't in the Swanky Palace or the Green

Frog either. But when they entered the Silver Slipper's smoke-choked interior, Slocum immediately noted that the crowd that turned to face them at their entry was made up of more miners than in the other two bars.

"Stubben!" Cribbs shouted, and drew the shotgun stock to his shoulder. The object of the lawman's attention was a big man at the end of the bar who, at the sight of them, had started to head for the back door.

"Hands up or die, mister!"

The man stopped, raised his hands, and turned. Slocum could see his face by then; it was the horse thief and killer from Owl Creek.

"That's him," Slocum said.

Cribbs by then had disarmed the man and warily, with his eye out for anyone that might jump in to save their friend, shoved him toward the front door. He motioned for Slocum to cover his back.

"Don't none of you try something foolish," Cribbs announced to the customers. "My finger gets itchy on this hair trigger, and I'll still have a round left for you after I blow his head plumb off. Stay seated. I don't need any help nor hindrance in this matter either."

Behind him, Slocum eased out the door into the cooler night, grateful for the fresh breath of air. His lungs filled with the fresh thin mountain air as he looked around for any sign of interference from anyone. Nothing.

"That was my horse you stole," he said, catching up with Cripps and the prisoner.

Stubben looked at him in disdain. "Too damn bad I stopped here."

"Right, too damn bad for you," Cribbs said, and shoved him down the street with the short Greener ready. "Slocum, I need you to sign some papers."

"Fine. I need to buy a wagon load of lumber in the morning and get back. I think I can find plenty of witnesses to the shooting up there."

"I'll tell the prosecutor. Mister, you even think about

running," Cribbs said, nudging the prisoner with the gun barrel, "you better have your prayers said 'cause you're paid for."

If it crossed Stubbens's mind, there was no sign; he went on up the stone steps into the courthouse ahead of them. Slocum glanced back at the saloons that faced the court-house. The pianos tinkled, and someone played a trumpet in one. Giddy laughter of soiled doves carried on the night air, along with the shouts of winning gamblers. It simply was another night in Prescott.

After the prisoner was jailed and the papers signed, Slo-cum went back to the wagon yard, found his own bedroll, and went back to the hay and slept until dawn. Then he dragged himself out, and washed his face and hands under a pump. He had the boy hitch his team while he went to eat. He found a cafe for a breakfast of coffee, eggs, ham, and sourdough biscuits to fill his empty gut.

The waitress gave him the directions to a sawmill with lumber for sale. In an hour, he had the wagon loaded with fresh-cut boards smelling of turpentine, and with the lumber paid for, was on his way. With the dun hitched to the tail-gate, he sat on the seat and wound his way out of town back up the road.

On the first flat he let the horses blow. Ahead, two other wagons of lumber were parked beside the road. He did not recognize any of the men standing around drinking whiskey from a shared brown bottle. They cast hard looks at him. When they finished the bottle, they tossed it off into the pines with a crash, and then they started in force across the road toward him.

Slocum saw the threat coming, and stepped off the seat in readiness. He reached into the box and extracted his Winchester, grateful that Stubben had not hocked or sold it. He levered a shell in and then swung the muzzle around.

"You gents looking for a lead belly?" He held the butt to his hip, and his action forced them to stop in the middle of the road.

"Where you going with that lumber?" the potbellied one with the mustache asked.

"Guess the same place where you're going."

"We've got the only contract to haul that up there to Owl Creek." The others nodded behind him.

"Free country, boys. I'm taking a lady some lumber she needs. Anyone want to stop me, step forward for his bullet."

"You thinking on bucking the four of us?" The man looked at his cohorts, and they nodded again.

"I think two of you will die if you force my hand. Anyone want to go first?"

"Let's talk."

"No talk, shuck those handguns in the dust. Do it with your fingers. Easy. Then step back." He motioned with the muzzle of the Winchester.

"You won't get by with this," the leader said. The men began to disarm with looks of anger on their faces.

Slocum walked over, bent down, and stuffed their handguns in his waistband. Then he motioned for them to step back.

"I'm going to start up the mountain. You better wait about thirty minutes to follow me, because I may be behind a bush up there and cut you down with this 44/40. You savvy good enough?" He pointed the long gun at the leader.

"Yeah, but you won't—all right, you've got the upper hand," the man said reluctantly.

Slocum walked back to the wagon, stepped up, undid the reins, and clucked to the horses. They had a hard pull ahead from there on. His greatest concern was to make it to Owl Creek alive and not get a bullet between his shoulder blades.

He heard the men grumbling as his team dropped into the collars and they wound up into the pines on the dusty road. Over his shoulder, he gave a last look at the angry teamsters. He'd drop their weapons off in the road up a ways. It was too bad that someone else was hauling lumber to Owl Creek. When he turned back to the front, the hair rose on the back of his neck. It would be a long drive to Owl Creek. *Get up, horses!*

6

Rain pounded him and bolts of lightning stabbed though the sky. Under his slicker, he huddled on the spring seat and picked his way toward the flickering lights of the Owl Creek settlement. Earlier he had stopped at Iron Mountain, but in the meantime, Mae had changed her mind about moving up to Owl Creek, and had sent him on. She'd found some miner with a pouch full of gold dust who'd promised to spend it all on her.

Since sundown the team had acted as if they knew the dark road. Still, with the lines in his cold hands, he looked uncertainly at the rushing creek several feet below the road to their left as they drew up the valley. If just one wheel dropped over that edge, he and the lumber would be in for a wet trip downstream.

At last, bone weary and tired, he pulled up in front of Hap's tent.

"That you, Slocum?" she asked, holding up the flap in one hand and the lamp in the other.

"Yes, ma'am," he said, finding some new energy at the sight of her and climbing down.

"Why didn't you stop and camp somewhere?" she asked, hurrying toward him.

59

"I didn't have the option. Besides, I tangled with some teamsters. Kramer's men, I guess."

"Did they hurt you?"

"No. Go back inside out of the rain," he said, waving her back.

"Oh, you've got your horse back. Good, I'll unsaddle him for you."

"I can do it. You're getting all wet." He frowned in her direction; she hadn't heard a thing he'd said.

"Never mind," she said. "You unhitch the team and I'll do the horse."

The rifle shot shattered the dreary night. The bullet's whine cut close by his ear as he struggled for his footing on the muddy ground. He'd seen the orange muzzle blast from the dark half-finished saloon next door as he dropped behind the horses.

"Get down!' he shouted to her, and drew his Colt.

He expected another report at any second. Gun in hand, he ducked under the team's heads. The falling mist was thick enough that he could hardly make out the outline of the structure where the shot had come from. Was the gunman still inside or had he already run? Every nerve in Slocum's body tingled. He pushed up the slope with slick mud under his soles and his trigger finger itching.

On the saloon's porch, his sodden boots squished as he stepped lightly toward the dark opening where the front doors would be hung. Not a sound came to his straining ears, except his horses snorting behind him and the splash of the runoff at the side walls. He held the pistol ready as he cautiously searched the dark room, but no one was inside. The shooter had fled.

"Are they gone?" she called out from the doorway behind him.

"Yes, that was a warning about how good they could get." He paused at the rear exit and studied the inky wet night beyond. Nothing had happened except for one well-placed rifle shot. It had been a message intended for him.

He understood such acts—the next slug would be in his gut if he didn't get out or stop the shooter first.

"Who do you think shot at you?" She caught up with him and hugged his arm.

"I imagine that pimple-faced Kid or his boss." He watched the shiny drops falling in front of him like diamonds in a sea of ink. If it was that pair, he'd learn soon enough.

"Mick Flannery?" she asked.

"He thinks he runs this town."

"He don't run me."

"No, but he told the doves in Iron City, if they came up here, he'd get fifty percent of their take."

"Whew, fifty percent. He's expensive."

"Damn expensive. Let me go put up the horses."

"I'm coming too."

"You don't listen good." He looked at her displeased.

"I listen well." She made him stop on the porch, and then she kissed him. Her lips were wet with the cold rain, and he tasted the passion of her mouth.

With the horses put up and the two of them back inside her large tent, she poured him coffee and fixed him a plate of leftover meat and potatoes. Rain drummed on the canvas, and drips from leaks in places added to the sound. Under the flickering lamp, he considered the heaping plate before him. His gut was trying to chew a hole in his spine, and he knew he needed the food. Still, the shot in the dark had finally made him hopping mad. Besides, they might have hit Hap. He fumed at the thought.

"You better eat." She put her hand on his shoulder and then sat down beside him. She had placed a bowl of apple dumplings and cream next to his plate.

"Anything else happen today?" He began to cut up the meat.

"The usual fistfights. Oh, yes, Slow Tom turned up drowned in the creek in his underwear."

"That's the drunk that you thought I found at the

claim?'' he asked, turning his head to look hard at her.

''Yes, that's him. No one knows anything about how he drowned. No bullet holes in him, though I felt a big knot on the top of his head.''

''Like he'd been struck before he drowned?'' Slocum asked.

''That's my guess.''

''Anyone see him come into camp wearing his underwear?''

''No. No one's seen him for a couple of days. Since before Charlie was murdered. Except you, I guess, and whoever hit him on the head.''

Slocum considered the matter. Since Tom was still in his underwear, he must have hidden out all day, then come into camp after dark.

''Oh, the saloon next door is going to be ready for business next week. The carpenters said so today and it's killing Flannery, I figure. His ain't half done.''

''They better guard it next door.''

''Who from?'' she asked with a frown.

''Flannery. Who else?''

''I guess I better tell them.'' She suddenly had a serious look.

''You better,'' Slocum said before tasting a forkful of the meat. ''Good food,'' he muttered between bites as the elk drew the saliva in his mouth. ''I guess they buried Tom already?''

''Sure, wrapped him in a blanket and sent him on his way. Why?''

''I guess I couldn't prove a thing. But I sure wonder how he got down here barefoot and in his underwear and ended up drowned.''

''I don't know.'' Her face paled.

Slocum considered his coffee. Lots of questions were unanswered, and they all pointed to Flannery and the Kid. But Slocum had no proof. Sure, Flannery could demand fifty percent from the whores, but there wasn't that much going on yet in Owl Creek to support them. Someone was behind that pair. He'd have to listen close. For now, all he heard was the rain on the tent, and she was anxious to know all about how he got his dun horse back.

"Where's that damn Frenchman and that pigtail help you sent him after?" Burns demanded.

"He ain't back yet?" Mick knew the boss was on a tear. He'd come to broach again the idea of a tent saloon, thinking maybe this time he could convince Burns to get the jump on the competition. And since Burns was short-handed, maybe he would go live at the McRoy claim. No one was there now.

"What's Default doing?" Burns demanded. "Gone for a damn boat ride?"

"I'll send the Kid in to find him."

"That Kid couldn't find his own ass."

"He almost got that Texan last night."

"Almost?"

"Yeah. It hadn't been raining so hard, he'd have nailed him."

"I thought you were going to take care of him yourself."

"I can't do everything." Mick took off his bowler and considered sailing it away in frustration. "I come up here with a good idea."

"A tent saloon again?" Burns shook his head as if the idea repulsed him.

"Yeah, well, it ain't such a bad idea. We could be selling booze and taking in gold."

"I want a real saloon. We hired them assholes to build me one. They said they could get it up in a few weeks," he raged.

"I can't do anything else with them bastards." Mick shook his head in defeat. Let Burns heap on his damn abuse. That bunch of lazy bastards couldn't build a shit-house in one day.

"You seen that China girl?" Burns asked, lowering his

voice and looking to see if Lucy was close enough to hear.

"I guess she's working at the cafe tent."

"You get a chance, you get her back up here."

"She wants her a maid, huh?" Mick pointed toward the tent.

"Yeah."

"What do you think if I set up a temporary bar?"

"Where?"

"On the damn porch of your uncompleted saloon. It's the only thing finished enough to use."

"Go ahead, but I don't like it."

"I'll be taking in lots of gold dust by dark." Damn, he had his permission at last!

"No class in that," Burns said. "Anyone can sell beer and whiskey."

"It'll make enough gold dust to pay some of the damn expenses you complain about."

"All right! Open the damn thing!" Burns glanced over as Lucy came out in a thin red duster that wrapped around her and showed her big dollar-sized nipples. "Find that girl," Burns said under his breath.

"I will, I will." Mick didn't concern himself for the moment about how he would get the China girl away from that woman and the Texan. They would be open for business and he'd be selling rotgut in two hours. He felt elated at finally convincing his boss to do it.

"We got another problem," he said, unsure how to explain everything.

"What's that?"

"I got rid of that drunk up at the mine. Figured he might talk."

"You did what?"

"No one saw us. Looked like an accident. He drowned in the creek."

"Who's watching the claim?"

"I figured maybe you should—well, go stay up there

until Default gets back.'' Flannery wanted to be out of the boss's reach as soon as possible.

"How long will that be?'' Burns demanded with a frown, as if in deep concentration.

"Not long. A couple of days, but it would keep anyone from jumping it. The cabin ain't half bad. I could send supplies and that Chinese girl up there.''

"Lucy, honey, pack a few things. We're going up in the hills a few days.''

"Hills? I hate hills.'' She made an aggravated face at Burns.

"You keep me informed,'' he said to Flannery. "That damn Default better get back here too.''

"I will. I will, boss.''

On his way downhill, Mick rubbed his hands together as he studied the early morning's scattered clouds. By damn, he would show Burns how to make money in a gold camp. Them that didn't spend it would lose their purses anyway. He knew his business. Hardly able to control himself, he almost ran downhill. He slammed open the door of the shed.

"Get your ass up, Kid. We've got work to do.''

The sleepy-eyed Kid sat up and yawned. "Yeah, what?''

"You go over and tell that Gabe Hammons I'm opening the bar in two hours and he's tending bar.''

"Huh?''

"Get up and get dressed. I ain't got time for no stupid questions.''

Dressed in his one-piece underwear, the Kid sat up and rubbed his face. Then he threw his legs over the edge of the cot and began to pull on his britches. His actions proved slow and made Mick impatient. But Mick stared out the window and fought to control his urge to explode. This was going to be his day.

At last, he heard the Kid stomp on his boots.

"I'm supposed to tell Gabe to come tend bar, huh?"

"Yes. Tell him and get back here. We've got lots of work to do."

"What about that Texan?"

"You missed him last night. You better wait till you're a better shot."

"It was raining like a son of bitch." The Kid made a sour face.

"You couldn't kill him at point-blank range," Mick snarled, and almost spat in the Kid's face.

"Oh, yeah, well, he's a dead sumbitch."

"Yeah, well, you listen, the boss wants that Chinese girl back."

"Shit, I'll kill that bastard and take her ass up there to him on a silver platter."

"You do that on your own damn time. Go find Gabe now."

The Kid plopped his wide-brim Boss of the Plains hat on his head and stomped outside grumbling to himself. Mick grinned after him. If he got the Kid fired up enough, he'd handle that Texan if he had to backshoot him. At the notion, Mick laughed to himself. Nothing was going to spoil his first day of being in business in Owl Creek.

7

Happy poured boiling water in the gray enamel pan set on the tabletop. Then she whipped the brush through it and began to stir the bristles in the soap mug. When it was loaded with suds, she deftly applied the lather to Slocum's face in the cool morning air.

"You sleep good enough?" she asked.

"I sure slept," he said, his mouth ringed in hot foam.

"Guess we were both too tired to do much more." The razor in her hand, she angled the blade as if deciding which side to start on. Her first sweep slid down his face, slicing away the stubble on his right cheek without a pull. She rinsed it off in the pan, then stropped the edge a time or two as if not satisfied with the keenness.

"I *was* tired," he admitted, not recalling much about the night before except falling asleep with her under his arm.

"Where were you raised?" she asked.

"Georgia."

"I thought I heard more drawl in your voice than Texas." She grinned at her discovery.

"I've been there the last few years driving cattle up to the rail heads in Kansas."

"Still, if you listen, you can tell a lot from a man's words about his origins. One time or other Texans all came from somewhere else."

"You came from Missouri," he said before she started in to shave some more. Her deft hand sliced off more foam and stubble.

"Right." She smiled again, cleaned off the blade, wiped it dry on a towel, and then went back for more.

"A mild drawl," he said.

"Yes. You ever been back home to Georgia?" she asked, scraping the skin beside his left ear.

"No, isn't anything left after the war."

"I loved Missouri. Grass grew waist-tall back there. I remember trees loaded with apples, rivers full of fish. I felt foolish as can be after I married and got out here. Why, I could hardly wait for the rain to make the Hassayampa River run water by down there at Wickenburg." She straightened to examine his face. "You're lucky. I never nicked you once today."

"I appreciate that." He wet the corner of the towel and then scrubbed away the soap as she watched him.

"I want to release you from our agreement," she said. "The men building the saloon next door will be done in a week, and they'll build my kitchen."

"I'm not good enough?" he asked, and stopped scrubbing with her Turkish towel to hear her answer.

"Oh, Slocum," she cried out loud. "I don't want you killed for my sake. You've got those teamsters riled up, and someone shot at you last night. I don't want you hurt."

"You let me worry about being hurt."

"I can't." She shook her head in defeat.

"I've met tougher men than Mick, that Kid, and a few teamsters. They'll forget it."

"No, they won't."

"Then by gawd, they'll wish they had."

"If I said help me load up and we'll go somewhere else, would you do it?"

"I don't run easy."

"Neither do I. But I can't see getting you shot or hurt minding my business."

"Then don't worry. I've lived this long, and one bullet don't make a good battle."

"What are you going to do today?"

"Unload the lumber. It will take two more trips back to Prescott to get enough up here for the frame, I figure."

"That many?" She swept her hair back from her face.

"It may take more."

"Can I help?" she asked.

"No, you run the cafe here."

"Hey, Happy, I got you a fat elk out here," a man in buckskins said, ducking to enter the back of the tent.

"That's Sam Duggan, my meat hunter," she said as the tall man came down the aisle toward them. "I sure need fresh meat today," she said to Duggan.

The two men were introduced and then shook hands; she went for coffee as they sat down.

"Hunting good up here?" Slocum asked.

"Fair. Lots of folks scouring these canyons scare the elk off, though. Several deer and some bear around close. She said you were going to help her get a building up?"

"That's my plan."

"How come you ain't prospecting?" Duggan asked.

"I've been working a silver claim down in the Dragoons all winter. I'm not anxious to start another."

"Digging rocks ain't for me neither. As long as the hunting lasts, guess I'll keep it up. She told me some fella stole your horse."

"Got him back. The thief is in the Prescott jail."

"They'll let him go. Should hang all them horse thieves."

"Holding him for murdering a man up here too."

"They need a good miners court up here. Take the law into their own hands and resolve things." The man behind the graying red beard filled his pipe, offered Slocum some tobacco, and then put it away when Slocum shook his head. "No lawyers and that legal stuff—just facts and a fast execution."

"Guess you've seen it work?"

"Yeah, I seen it work in a buffalo-skinning camp. Out on the prairie miles from towns and judges. Anyone stole another's things, we held court right there and decided guilt or innocence. Took an ax and chopped off one finger for a minor offense, two for bigger ones. You stole a man's horse, we hung you on the wagon tongue. We had little trouble the whole two years." He ignited the old briar and drew on it. The sweet thick smoke was strong in Slocum's nose.

"You must have worked the southern herd," Slocum said.

"Yeah, cashed in my last hides at Fort Griffin."

"Gone now, aren't they?"

"Ain't enough buffalo left in this country to fill a small farmyard. Shame too. I loved them shaggy bastards. You must have hunted some."

"Some." Slocum absently studied Hap as she brought the coffeepot down the aisle. He had seen lots of buffalo. He remembered the stink of spent gunpowder and the feel of a hot Sharp's rifle in his hands. The grassland before him had been covered with mounds of dead buffalo, waiting for the skinners. He knew why Duggan spoke reverently of those days; so did he. Never again. He shut his eyes to the memory.

"Coffee hot and fresh," Hap announced.

"We must have crossed trails in them years," Duggan said with a frown.

"Probably did."

"I'll place you somewhere," Duggan said, and busied himself holding out his cup. "You know, if we keep on, in a few years won't be nothing left to hunt. No elk, deer, or bear."

"Probably won't be, the way this country is sure filling

in,'' Slocum agreed as he looked through the steam that rose off his fresh cup.

"Mick's opening his saloon on the porch this afternoon,'' a miner said, his head stuck in the tent. Then he hurried on to tell others, excited with the news.

"I could use a good drink,'' Duggan said, and set the coffee cup down. "I may just stick around a while.''

"May be,'' Slocum said.

"May be?'' The hunter cocked a bushy eyebrow at him.

"Yes, may be a good drink and may be tainted. Mick is not the most savory man in this camp.''

"I understand,'' Duggan said. Then he rose, excused himself, and left them after she paid him for the elk.

"It's a fat cow elk this time,'' she said to Slocum when they were alone again.

"You'll need it for the hungry men.''

"I better get to cooking too,'' she said, and popped up to her feet.

"I'll unload the lumber.'' He'd put it off long enough.

Up the street of mud, Flannery was filled with excitement watching the barrels of beer and whiskey being rolled onto the porch. He'd hired six miners to help set up, with the promise of unlimited beer for their labor. He was about to crack a bottle open and start on it. His every nerve tingled as he directed the men in their work.

Gabe, the bartender, worked unpacking glasses and stacking them on the rough board shelves that were hastily set up on boxes. Mick nodded his approval of the setup so far. Then he spotted the Kid at the corner leaning against the building.

"Ride into Prescott and find that dumb Frenchman,'' Mick said. "I need those Chinese diggers up here and right away. The boss is on my ass about the deal.''

"Why, it'll take all day and night to go up there and back.''

"That's what I pay you for.'' Mick's breath began to

race out his nose as he fought down his impatience.

"All right, I'm going."

You better. That damn Kid could make him so mad, he could hardly contain himself. Where was that nosy Texan Slocum? Probably climbing on that voluptuous Happy. Man, *he'd* like to climb on her. He closed his eyes, and when he opened them, the Kid was still standing there.

"What's wrong?"

"Old Man Kramer's coming. He looks mad as hell too."

"I'll handle that old bastard—get your horse and ride." He gave the Kid a shove to send him on his way. What did Kramer want? The old German looked on the prod.

"What's wrong?" Flannery asked, searching around to be certain they weren't overheard.

"Dat gawdamn cowboy brought a wagon load of lumber up here."

"So?"

"I pay you dat money so I am the only one brings lumber up here!"

"I'll handle it."

"Yeah, well, maybe you in cahoots with him!"

"I ain't in cahoots with no one."

"Then you stop him or I don't pay you another gawdamn dime!"

"I hear you." Shit, now that damn Texan was about to spoil something else. What else could happen? Nothing else to do but get rid of him.

"Go back to peddling your lumber—he ain't no threat."

"He damn sure is!"

"Kramer! Let me handle it!" Flannery shouted.

"By gawd, you better and quick."

Mick watched the old German stalk up the main street. They were putting a sign up on the other bar in town. Silver King Saloon. Big black letters—shit, he'd have a naked lady painted on his front sign. Have to find an artist somewhere to do it though.

He looked down the street. Where in the hell was that

damn Slocum going with his empty wagon? Probably going back to Prescott for more lumber. Damn him anyway! Mick clenched his fists tight at his sides. He had to stop him. Too much depended on that and he had no time left.

8

Slocum lost no time heading out of camp. The less commotion he made, the fewer problems he would have. A hug and quick kiss for Hap, and then he was driving the black horses down the valley, headed for the grade in the west. He checked over his shoulder to be certain he wasn't being followed.

A powerful explosion on the hillside, and the resulting cloud of dust, only hurried the horses down the road. The empty wagon jolted around on the ruts, but he planned to let the horses blow at the grade. So he urged the blacks on as they wound their way above the creek, drawing the stares of the prospectors working in the stream, some of whom waved. Many of them ate their meals at Hap's place and knew him.

At the base, he drew the team down to a jog. When he looked back for the last time, timber and the mountainside obscured all but the smoke of campfires over the treetops. He turned his attention to driving his team. He planned to be in Iron Mountain by dark. By his calculations, all of Kramer's wagons were in camp still being unloaded, so they wouldn't be on the road or able to block his way. Not

74

that he feared a few rough-hided teamsters, but it was better to avoid any confrontation—get his load of lumber and get back. Three loads would have to do for Hap's building. He stamped his boot soles on the wagon floor to increase the circulation in his feet. Then an idea struck him. He'd hire some other wagons in Prescott to help bring in his load. That would ensure Hap all her needed lumber. The idea pleased him as the sun dropped behind the far horizon and shone copper red on the bald peaks.

Good country—they simply needed to rid it of Mick and others like the Kid so honest folks could get on with their prospecting. But how could he do it? There had to be a way—all he needed was a plan. He shrugged off his concern for the moment; an idea would come to him.

Four hours later and after sunset, he reached Iron Mountain and reined up his team at the wagon yard. He planned to spend the night, then push on at first light. When his horses were rubbed down, watered, and grained, he headed for the main lights for some food and a drink. He climbed on the porch of the saloon with some effort and stopped. The sound of a tinny piano from inside made him smile. He raised his high-crown hat, swiped his gritty forehead on his sleeve, and replaced the hat. Then he adjusted the six-gun on his hip out of habit, and pushed inside.

A few miners turned to look in his direction, then turned back to either the girls on their arms or their drinks. The roulette wheel whirled, and a few men leaned over it tensely.

"What'll it be, cowboy?" the barkeep asked.

"Good whiskey. You got any?"

"Bottle and bond. Damn good rye. Cost you fifty cents a shot. How much you want?"

"Two shots. Straight."

"Coming up." The man made a swipe under the counter, came up with a bottle, showed the label to him, and then poured the whiskey in a glass. "Drink to your health," he said, and picked up the silver dollar Slocum laid on the bar.

"I may need that luck." He considered the whiskey, and then sipped some of it. The sharp liquor cleared out some of the road dust from his throat and warmed his ears. Not bad—not the best, but better than the usual rotgut served in such places.

"Any place I can get a meal this time of night?" he asked the barkeep when he came by to refill some mugs with frothy beer.

"Steak, bread, and beans."

"Sounds good enough." Slocum glanced over his shoulder and spotted an empty table. "I'll take it over there," he said, indicating the table.

"Coming up," the man said, and went to fill the mugs.

His back to the wall, Slocum settled in the chair and observed the rough-and-tumble prospectors in the barroom. None of them acted interested in him, and Mae was nowhere in sight.

"Here's your food," a youth said, and placed the heaping plate of food before him.

"How much?" Slocum asked.

"Fifty cents."

"Bring me a cold beer to wash it down," he said, and produced sixty cents from his pocket.

"Yes, sir."

Slocum cut the strips of browned steak with the knife, pausing to taste a piece. He chewed thoughtfully, and decided the notion of the meal wasn't a bad idea. Finished with the bite, he tossed down the rest of the whiskey. He planned to sleep only a few hours and be under way.

His meal completed, he finished the beer and rose. The notion of getting some sleep was on his mind as he left the bar. Outside on the porch, he let his eyes grow accustomed to the darkness.

The flash of red-orange gunfire cut the night, and the impact of the bullet spun him around. Slocum felt the hot lead knife into his shoulder as he rolled off the porch and more shots followed. But he knew there was no sense fighting for the Colt pinned under his body. He'd misjudged his enemy—and now he was helpless.

He fought for his consciousness as the shock of the wound began to set in. Where was that backshooter? Would he come by and finish him off? Slocum rose and began to crawl. The shooting had spooked some of the horses at the hitch rack, and they milled about in the street, stepping on their reins.

No clear sight of the shooter yet. The saloon crowd was cautiously holding back at the door, not wanting to rush out into any cross fire. Slocum tried to focus his attention across the street where the shots had come from.

At last he managed to draw his Colt in his left hand. The warm flood of blood soaked his shirt and vest. He rose unsteadily to his knees, tucking the hurt shoulder and right arm in close. On his feet at last, he set out for the dark space between the two stores opposite him. He had the hammer back, but he doubted his accuracy with his off hand. Despite his intense effort, his vision began to waver. Next, his knees buckled and he went facedown. The Colt went off in his hand, and he tasted the gun smoke and then the dirt.

"Get Doc," someone shouted.

Slocum could feel the Colt being pried from his fingers. Helpless to do a thing, he felt them roll him over on his back. Someone held a light over him that looked miles away. Then he felt it all slipping from him. He began a spiral plunge into a deep well. The fall was end over end, and he never found the bottom before he passed out and all went black.

Flannery was bone tired when he reached Owl Creek long past midnight. It was still before sunup, and no one was on the road. A coyote howled up in the timber, and then ran off with his pack yipping. Above him, the dim light of the stars lighted the peaks as he dropped from the saddle, turned the horse in without unsaddling him, and stumbled

inside the shack. That bastard Texan was taken care of—
no more bitching from Kramer about him bringing in lumber, or from the boss about his interfering. After Flannery
slept some, he'd take the Chinese bitch from that Hap
woman and deliver her ass to Lucy. He tossed his bowler
aside, dropped belly-down on the bunk, and fell asleep.

At dawn Flannery dragged himself up. He splashed water
on his face to wake up, dried his face on a sour stiff towel,
and then set out. First he went by and kicked awake the
sleeping guard he'd hired to watch the porch bar. Damned
old drunk—should have known he would be worthless. He
pulled down his vest, straightened his shoulders, and kept
on walking and looking for the Chinese bitch. About this
time she went to work, and he aimed to intercept her.

Then he saw her coming down the road in the long shadows. How good could it be? Slocum gone and Lady Luck
bringing him the little gal. She shuffled along with her
hands inside her sleeves against the morning cold. Careful
not to let her see him, he stood back in the shadows under
the boughs of the fragrant pine.

In an instant he stepped out and had her. One hand
clamped off her mouth to muffle her screams. The other
went around her waist as he dragged her back under the
tree. When she was facedown with his knee in her back,
he used her kerchief to gag her. Then he stripped off his
belt and used it to tie her hands. He ignored her efforts to
kick and fight him. What could a skinny bitch do to him?
Nothing.

He slung her over his shoulder and hurried to his shack.
That no one saw him was all that concerned him. Out of
breath, he pushed inside the shack and spilled her on the
cot. Her slanted eyes were wide in fear as he stopped to
grin at her, pleased with himself over his success. He
searched for some rope to tie her up with until he could
move her up to the claim. Too bad that Hap woman would
have to do all her own work from now on. Things were
going much better for him for a change.

He found the cord in a trunk, crossed the room, and tied her ankles. Then he considered her, and an evil grin crossed his face as he pinched her breasts. They were small rock-hard knobs, he discovered as she winced in pain at his hard grasp. He wrinkled his nose at her in disgust—he liked a real woman with real tits. Ignoring her pleading look, he rolled her over and replaced his belt with a fresh rope around her wrists.

"You can stay gagged a while," he said, turning her back over. Then he straightened, combed his dark hair with his fingers, and caught his breath back. His heart hurt him; he tried to ignore it as he looked smugly into her pale face, amused at the shocked expression.

"I don't want you screaming your damn head off. I'll be back later. I may use your skinny ass myself when I come back before I take you up to the claim."

Flannery locked the shack door with a padlock. No sense letting someone stumble in and find her. Then he hurried up to the saloon. Lots of things to tell the boss about later. The makeshift saloon had made lots of money the first night, Slocum the troublemaker was dead, and that Chink bitch was his prisoner. He paused and drew in his breath. Damn high country took his breath a lot when he over-exerted himself. He held his hand against his shirt; his heart pounded hard inside his chest—he'd get it back in a minute. The wave of dizziness passed. He hurried on.

9

"Slocum, can you hear me?" Mae asked.

"Yes," he managed from his dark world. His thoughts were cobwebbed by things he barely could see, and the rest he could not make out at all. On top of that, his strength felt drained away.

"You took a slug in the right shoulder. The shooter got away. No one saw him—well, Charlie Johnson said he did. Said that he wore a bowler. Saw him run out the alley, but it was so damn dark all he saw was an outline."

"Good enough," came from Slocum's lips more weakly than he ever thought possible.

"Doc says he's got the bleeding stopped. You should start mending. He's giving you laudanum for the pain."

"Thanks. It has me pretty crazy in the head, I guess."

"Anything I can do for you?"

"I'm fine." He tried to force a smile, but it hurt him. Everything hurt him as he lay on his back, with the smell of the powerful disinfectant in his nose and a complete loss of strength—a situation that made him edgy. To be so helpless meant he would be too vulnerable if the shooter came back to finish the job.

"How did you get in such a mess?" she asked.

"I can't be certain of a thing. Might be that Irishman . . ." He knew the medicine had taken ahold of him, and he slipped off into a dark abyss.

Slocum blinked his eyes against the bright light. He stood in the hot sunlight in the center of the street of some unfamiliar Southwest town. No grass, nothing green, but some lacy mesquite trees in between the buildings. He blinked as he studied the empty boardwalks on his left and right. Where was everyone? His spurs made a soft jingle as he strode down the hard-packed caliche, swept clean of dust by the fiery wind.

Dark piles of horse apples dotted the ground at the hitch racks. Still fresh, he decided as he kept walking. Where was he headed and what was his purpose? No way to know, but he had to be on his guard. There was a threat in this town—one he would only know when it focused on him. Man? Gunfighter? Bounty hunter? Who wanted him?

The hot wind seared his eyes. No sign of a soul. He kept walking—the street went on and on forever. Why, there must be blocks and blocks of adobe buildings with faded signs, a weathered boardwalk on each side, and empty hitch rails. He dried his palm on the side of his pants. He tested the Colt in his holster. Free enough. Loaded to the gate, he knew. He kept walking as if compelled by an unseen hand pushing him.

To his right, a loose bat-wing door slapped back and forth in a noisy squeak. Nothing . . . no one. What was he doing in this street—this hellhole?

Then he saw someone step into the street. He wore a black frock coat and a wide-brim hat that shaded his face. Who was he? Compelled to keep walking, Slocum rolled the fingers in his gun hand at his side. Filled with a dread, he still could not make out who this man coming toward him really was.

The stranger went for his gun. Slocum went for his and

thumbed back the hammer. It fell on a dud. The dreaded click sounded so loud it hurt his ear. He raised the pistol up to eye level, and the second round failed to go off.

The other man was laughing by this time—as if he knew about the duds, as if he'd planned it all the time and was making no effort to shoot. As if he waited—waited for Slocum to try all five of the loaded cylinders. Then the shooter took aim, and the blast of smoke belched out of his revolver, and Slocum staggered backward for a long ways, hit in the shoulder. He fell on his back, and the man stood over him mocking and laughing at his plight.

Who was the shooter? Slocum couldn't see his face for the glare of the sun in his eyes. Who'd shot him?

"Wake up, Slocum. Wake up, you were screaming," Mae said with urgency.

He tried to raise up and see where he was at, still thinking he lay there in the street. It was dark, except for a small lamp on the side table that illuminated the room and cast a large shadow of her form on the wall. No street, no gunman that he did not know. He felt grateful for the wool blanket over him, for the room was cool. She wore a blanket over her shoulders.

"You were dreaming, I guess," she said, busy tucking him under the covers.

"Guess I was." He felt bound up by the bandages, and hardly had the strength to even stir. His whole shoulder was on fire. Disturbed by his memories of the dream, he considered his fragile condition as he stared at the ceiling and her flickering shadow while she filled a spoon with more laudanum for him. The burning grew deeper, and he knew the medicine meant more dreams—not dreams, but nightmares.

Bursting with pride, Flannery grasped the lapels of his coat as he stood beside the saloon porch in the early morning sunshine. Miners were making their way to the Arnold woman's tent for breakfast. He needed twenty percent of her take; maybe he would whip her in line next. He'd eliminated his worst source of trouble—the cowboy. Plugged him in the heart, and no one could tie him to the murder either. Things were going more the Flannery way, the way he liked it. The saloon made money, and his boss up there sat on a real gold mine.

If that damn Default didn't get back with those pigtails soon—he'd go find him and kill him too. He should never have sent the Kid after him. That boy got dumber and more rebellious by the day. Flannery should have gone himself. If the Kid wasn't careful, he'd end up with old Slow Tom in the creek. Only thing Flannery had left to do was haul that China girl out to the claim, and he'd be caught up for the first time in weeks. It was the next day, and he still had her prisoner in his shack. Maybe later he could wrap her in some blankets and get her out of town so no one would know what had happened to her—a minor problem anyway. No one missed a damn Chinese. With Slocum dead, no one stood in his way. He should have done it sooner—handled it himself.

"You watch this place until Gabe gets here," he said to the saloon guard seated in the chair in the shade.

"How about some food?" the man called Evers asked.

"Yeah, it'll be noon before Gabe comes. You go over and eat at the tent, but be quick about it." He drew in a breath. He had no relief for the man except himself. "I'll watch things. But hurry."

"Yes, sir." Evers nodded, adjusted his galluses as he rose, and set out at a trot for the tent. Flannery watched him move. The man at least knew the value of his time.

The first night they must have cleared at least a hundred ounces of gold dust and some cash money. He could hardly wait until Evers came back so he could go up to the shack to count the second night's take. One thing he had learned in two nights of business. Those muckers were getting more dust out of the ground up there than they were letting on. Why, he'd have the damn saloon paid for before the lazy bastards he'd hired had it built. Where were they anyway? He scowled to himself—they were probably eating breakfast at the Arnold woman's place. Oh, he needed a share in her take badly.

He climbed in the guard's chair, and greeted the passing miners trudging up the road for their breakfast. Many only ate two meals a day, breakfast and then supper. The richer ones ate lunch—he'd watch them closer. He let his feet stretch out in front of him, and he crossed his shoes. A man could deduce a lot of things when he wasn't under pressure.

If Default and the Kid didn't show up by dark, he'd go find and kill both of them.

"Hey, Mick!" a bearded passerby shouted. "Hope you ain't run out of beer!"

"We ain't."

"Good thing. The thought will keep me going all day."

"I hope you get a double a handful of gold today," he shouted after the man.

"Maybe I'll strike the bonanza!" the man yelled back over his shoulder.

"Yeah." Boy, he could use the bonanza himself. But he wasn't doing bad. Kramer was paying him twenty percent, and the merchants Puley and Davis were on the list for the same. Wasn't hurting them any—they just charged the customers more—and where else could the miners get their stuff?

Once a week, he went around and collected his share. He collected from everyone in business but the Arnold woman. He had studied her carefully. The miners worshipped her ass. She'd been there before he and Burns arrived. There was damn sure power in being the only attractive woman in camp and the one who fed the others. She was not a person he felt he could whip into line without raising the ire of the whole camp. Besides, they needed a place to eat to be able to work.

Still, he considered her operation as he recrossed his

shoes the other way and nodded to a couple more saloon customers passing by. She must sell several hundred dollars worth of meals each day. Twenty percent of that was money he needed for himself. Not Harvey Burns. It would be no one's money but his own. It was his insurance policy. When things got too hot, he could light out for parts unknown, and not have to stay in some hellhole like Yuma because he was too broke to leave and had to ride Burns's coattails.

No, someday when he was ready, Mick Flannery would leave Owl Creek on a stagecoach with his pockets full of money. His thoughts went back to his prisoner. How would he get that damn girl out to the claim? He'd think of a way. Or simply wait until night—that might be the best.

Burns would be beside himself if Flannery didn't show up until after midnight. Nothing for his boss to do up there but play with Lucy's butt. He grinned to himself. He needed a setup like that, like Burns had. Some sweet voluptuous thing at his beck and call to jump in bed whenever he had the notion, and a dozen Mick Flannerys to do his bidding. Yeah, that would be the way to live. He settled his back in the large chair. By gawd, he'd do that somewhere when he got through at Owl Creek.

Evers was hurrying back. Flannery rose and stretched his tight muscles. All that riding to Iron Mountain two nights ago and little sleep since had made him sore.

"Get to eat?" he asked.

"Yeah. Guess what?"

"What?"

"Someone wounded that cowboy that hung out with her. They did it two nights ago up at Iron Mountain."

"Wounded him?" Flannery asked, taken aback at the man's words. How in the hell could that be—*wounded him?*

"Yeah, a fella came from there. Hap ain't serving lunch

today. Going there and see about him. Guess she was sweet
on him, don't you guess?''

"He was alive, huh?" Flannery studied her big tent
down the way. Maybe he'd die from the infection. Or Flannery would do the job right the next time. *Oh, damn.*

10

"Slocum, can you hear me?"

He tried to open his eyes. He knew from behind his lids that sunlight flooded the room. The medication had confused him, but some things he realized, and the voice calling him was Hap Arnold.

"Hi," he managed with a small smile as he saw her face looking down surrounded by a great halo of light.

"I met Mae," she said. "She told me what happened. Oh, I feel so bad. If I had just—"

He lifted his good hand and reached for hers. "Don't trouble yourself. I'll mend in time. Nothing serious cut up, according to the doc."

"But I feel so guilty. This is all my fault."

"Hap, it ain't. You go back and run your business. I'll be along in a few days with the lumber."

"No! Forget the lumber. I'll buy it from Kramer."

"At four times the price that I can haul it out of Prescott. No, don't do that." He raised his head off the pillow in frustration over his condition.

"I won't have anyone else hurt because of me."

"Hap, you'll think different in a week or so. Those boys

get the Silver King Saloon done, you'll listen to reason.''

"Slocum, what can I do for you?'' She dropped on her knees beside the bed and clasped his good hand in both of hers.

"I'll be fine here for a few days. Mae will look after me. Then I'll move up there—if you want me?''

" 'Want you' '' She closed her eyes and then pressed her forehead to his. "I won't know what to do until you can be moved. I mean, I shut down for lunch today to come here. And another thing. Lou Wee is missing too.''

"Flannery and that pock-faced Kid are behind that.'' He wanted to throw aside the blanket and go find the pair.

"Slocum, don't get so upset. I'm sorry I brought you all my grief. I intended to cheer you up.'' She looked down at him with wet lashes that glistened.

She kissed him on the face and then rose. She blew her nose softly, and went to the window.

"Speaking of the Kid,'' she said. "He's riding by on his paint and Default's with him. He's driving a wagon load of Chinese headed for Owl Creek.''

Slocum drew a deep breath. Cheap labor for some purpose. He closed his eyes, trying to figure out what they intended to do with the workers. Maybe he would learn soon enough—it was such an effort to simply hold his eyes open.

"I'll be back to check on you in three days,'' she promised.

"I'll be ready to go with you then,'' he said, uncertain if he would be able to go back with her then or not.

"We'll see.''

"Hap, I have money in my pants. Take some and go by and pay my bill on the team at the livery.''

"I'll handle it,'' she said, and dismissed his offer. "I paid the doctor, and I offered Mae money, but she turned it down. Said she owed *you* money.''

"She don't. I can—'' He stopped as Hap bent over him, swept the hair back from his forehead, and then kissed him.

"You rest and get well." She looked at him hard for a reply, a promise.

"I will."

"You have to."

Unable to keep his eyes open another second, he slipped off into sleep. His nightmares returned too.

Flannery studied the wagon winding its way up the valley. Then he recognized the paint horse coming along beside it. Flannery was en route to check on Gabe, who should be setting up for the evening's business. He intended to discuss hiring Evers as the second barkeep. The young boys Gabe had working the saloon were dependents of the miners, too young to do much work in the ground. They could serve drinks for two bits and a few tips a night. But the way the business was building, a second good man could help. The Kid could do the job of the night guard—earn his thirty bucks a month.

Flannery hiked down the road. No sense having those damned Chinks in camp. He'd better stop them and send them on up to Burns.

"Took you long enough," he said as Default reined up. Flannery looked over the bunch of Chinamen, who stood up and bowed their heads for him.

"Hard to get them," Default grumbled, sounding in a bad mood.

"No sense stopping here. Get some rice and some salt pork from up at the Davis store. Tell him to put it on my bill, and then take them up to the claim. Burns is up there waiting for you."

The Kid had dismounted, and was hiking up in his bull-hide chaps and looking around. "What am I supposed to do?"

"Go get some sleep. You're the saloon night watch-man."

"Ah, shit," he swore, and made a face.

Flannery stepped over close, handed him the padlock

key, and under his breath warned him, "Don't you mess with that China girl either. She's tied up there. I'm taking her up to Lucy when it gets dark enough."

"Yeah?" He curled his lip as if he didn't care what he said.

"You heard me." Flannery had to control his temper and not backhand him.

Then Flannery turned his attention to Default. "You ready?"

The Frenchman rubbed his ratty mustache with his palm, considering the bar set up on the porch. There was no mistaking his need. Flannery stepped up, went around behind the bar, pulled out a pint of rye, and returned.

"It comes out of your pay," he said, and handed it to the sly, smiling Default.

"Take it out." With a disgusted look, Default considered his passengers, who were chattering back and forth in their own language. He shook his head, stuck the bottle between his legs, released the brakes, and then clucked to the small team of mustangs.

Flannery decided to go with him for the supplies. They'd need enough to feed them damn slant-eyes for a month at least. Couple hundred-pound sacks of rice—he'd get that hunter Duggan to take them some meat up there.

The chattering of the workers in the wagon ahead sounded like magpies to Flannery as he hiked after it, stepping over the wet spots and mud holes. Gawd, he was glad he didn't have to work that bunch of monkeys. He'd let that Frenchman do that. He could bribe Default with whiskey or the promise of it and get him to do the job—thank gawd.

In front of the Davis mercantile tent, he spotted the hunter Duggan bringing in two deer carcasses. He waved him over.

"Hey, I'll need a couple deer a week up at the new mine past the Indian rock on Clover Creek."

"That Charlie's old claim?" Duggan asked as if considering the matter.

"Not now. Ah, Mr. Burns claims it."

"Kinda fancy guy, ain't he, for prospecting and mining work?"

"He'll need a couple of deer a week up there to feed this lot. You selling game?"

Duggan reined up his stout horse and looked over at the Chinese, who were now quiet and hunkered down. Then he nodded.

"May have to bring you bear meat. Deer and elk getting scarce close by. Anyway, them Chinamen think bear meat gives them big hard-ons."

"They don't need that up there." Flannery frowned at the notion.

"Take it or leave it," Duggan said.

"All right—bear meat." He didn't like the man's attitude, nor his comments about that being Charlie's mine. Charlie was in the ground—he didn't need a damn mine. A man Duggan's age ought to have learned to keep his mouth shut about such things. He could ask Slow Tom about it in the hereafter if he wasn't careful.

"Don't forget to bring it," Flannery said under his breath, and then he went into the mercantile tent with his head down.

In thirty minutes, the wagon was loaded with food, shovels, picks, wheelbarrows, buckets, spool of rope, canvas for shelters, and explosives. Flannery took off his derby and scratched the thin hair on top of his head as he watched the wagon wag its way down past the Arnold woman's tent.

He noticed her dismount and tie up the dun horse at the hitch rack. If Slocum had been dead, she'd not have come back so fast. Damn, maybe he could hope that the son of a bitch would die from complications. He knew he had shot him in the chest close to the heart. Tough bastard—next time he'd cut his head off and be sure he had killed him. He must be laid up, though—she hadn't brought him back.

So he'd be no problem for the time being. One good thing. Slocum couldn't haul any lumber in his shape, and Kramer couldn't cuss Flannery over that.

With a hard exhale through his nose, he headed back to the shack. He seldom took his meals in a cafe. He'd once had food poisoning and almost died. Since then he ate hardtack and canned sardines and things like canned corned beef. He wasn't taking any chances on getting that sick again.

Of course he'd never heard of anyone getting sick eating the Arnold woman's food. His belly ached at the recall of the time he got so sick. Ate only browned flour for five days, and took lots of Dr. Crain's Blackberry Root tonic to stop the diarrhea. His butt had been on fire, and he'd needed a powder puff to wipe it. He sighed at the notion as he glanced over at the carpenters working on the saloon.

Maybe a good case of diarrhea would wake them up. Purge their lazy systems.

"Morning, Flannery," the lead man, Rogers, said.

"You men going to finish the roof this week?" he asked, looking at the fresh lathing over the rafters.

"We should."

"See that you do," he said, and turned to head for his shed.

"Set us out some roofing nails," Rogers said after him. "I tried to get some out of the shack, but the door was locked."

"I will," Flannery said. So they'd been up snooping around his shack. Good thing that he'd locked it up. Where was the Kid? Hell, he'd given him a key to get inside. Maybe they didn't know the Kid had gone up there.

His good brass lock lay on the ground. He picked it up with a frown. When he tried the door, it was barred on the inside.

"Open up!" he shouted.

"Yeah, yeah," the Kid said. "I'm coming."

Flannery frowned and looked around, wondering what

was taking him so long. Then the door finally opened, and he saw the Kid was standing there stark naked with a big pink erection.

On the bed, he saw the small exposed butt of the China girl. Her hands were tied to each side of the cot. Her slender legs were bare, and he figured in a second what the Kid had been doing. He flew into a rage.

"You stupid punk!" From his hind pocket, he drew his leaded blackjack and began to swing it down on the Kid's arms, which he held up in protest, backing away, until the blows hurt him so bad that he dropped to his knees. With his rage in full flame, Flannery repeatedly slashed him on his head and shoulders.

Sobbing and crying, the Kid was beyond defending himself. Flannery finally silenced him with repeated blows to the head. His victim at last sprawled facedown on the floor. Flannery was out of breath, and his lungs ached and his heart pounded so hard his head swam. He dropped his butt to the other cot and stared at the girl. She turned away to avoid his gaze.

Stupid boy must have intended to bugger her. Maybe he had been doing that to her when Flannery knocked. Damn Kid probably had screwed sheep before too. Wonder how she would be. He'd not had a Chinese hooker in years, not since he was in St. Louis. His breathing began to come easier, and his heart had stopped hurting him so much.

He crossed the room and untied her hands. With one hand he jerked her around and then up to a sitting position. She cowered up in the corner of the bed and looked at him with concern.

"Lay down on your back," he said, pointing at the bed.

"No," she said in a small voice.

"Lay down or . . ." He stuck the blackjack in her face, and then he pointed at the kid. "I'll do the same to you that I did to him."

She began to obey, but slowly, as if uncertain. Her slanted eyes looked at him in dark suspicion as she scooted

herself cautiously down the cot. Conscious of her naked-
ness, she pulled down the tail of her blouse to cover her
exposed waist and below.

"Take it off," he said, hanging his coat and vest on the
chair. A wave of excitement made the skin on his back
crawl. It was time he had some pleasure.

She hesitated. He gave her a hard look and made a start
toward her. She shook her head hard and hurried to comply.
Her hand trembled as she rushed to remove her blouse.
Then she held her hands on top of each other over her pubic
area as she lay back on the bed.

He took off his pants, his blood beginning to surge at
the notion of taking her. It had been a long time—too long
since he'd had a woman. He'd been looking at Lucy too
long as well.

Undressed, he put a knee on the cot, and pulled on his
growing manhood to stiffen it. He moved her hands aside
to see her crotch. No pubic hair, only a seam—how old
was she? *Old enough to bleed, old enough to butcher.* He
wasn't going to let that stop him. Besides he recalled that
Chinese women didn't have a lot of body hair.

"Girl, you better be good at this or I'm going to beat
you up like I did him. You savvy?"

She gave him a quick nod as her face paled under her
almond skin. He pushed her legs apart. His breath shortened
and sharp pains struck inside his chest. Damn high country
anyway, it did that to him. The hurt did not stop him. He
moved in closer and dropped his belly down between her
beanpole legs. The ropes under the cot protested at his
weight.

He tried to force the nose of his rod into her. She stifled
a cry.

"Kinda tight fit," he said, greedy with his desire to enter
her. He squeezed the shaft in his fingers to make it stiffer,
and tried to drive it in her. She groaned in pain. It wouldn't
go in. Too tight. Was she sewn together? Then, to his dis-
may, he felt an explosion in his testicles and made a des-

perate effort to enter her, but her unyielding opening held him out. Too late, his seed spewed forth, and the very nose of his shaft ached as it remained painfully wedged just between the sides of her ungiving gates.

He closed his eyes. Damn, was she a virgin or something else? Maybe he would have to try her later. He glanced over at the moaning Kid, who had pushed himself up on his palms.

Quite a sight—the Kid's right eye was swollen shut, blood streaking down his face. He looked mighty pitiful. Maybe he'd learn to listen to orders. Flannery rose in disgust at his own failure, went to the washbowl, wrung out a washrag, and ran it over his privates, then dried them on the stiff towel. He tossed the washrag for her to clean herself. Sitting up, she caught it.

He watched her use the cloth to clean herself, occupied with the task as if in a private bath. He ignored the moans of the Kid, who sat on the dirt floor and held his head. Flannery busied himself putting on his own clothing.

"She gets done, you clean yourself up," Flannery told the Kid as he finished dressing. Still naked, she stepped around the Kid who was sitting in a daze on the floor and holding his sore head. Lou Wee picked up the towel. She smelled it, and then she put it back as if too dirty to use.

Flannery considered her. She'd not try to run away without her clothes. Besides, she had to eat something. He drew a deep breath as he studied her. He wasn't through with her. It had been a while since he'd been with a woman. He'd gotten too excited too fast was all.

"Clean him up," Flannery said to her.

She frowned.

"Clean him up," he repeated. "And don't put on any clothes or I'll tie your ass up again."

She nodded. He took some crackers and hard cheese to eat on the way. Why had he come so soon on top of her? Hell, he was tired of looking at the both of them.

"Don't mess with her!" he said at the door, pointing his

free hand at the Kid. He waited until he acknowledged his words. "Set a keg of roofing nails out for Rogers, and keep her hid in here."

He stepped outside, closed the door, and then took a big bite of the cheese and crackers. It wadded in his mouth. Why had he come so soon on top of her? And why did his chest and now his whole right arm hurt so bad all of a sudden? Must have strained some muscles. He pushed on his upper chest with his hand full of crackers. Damn the pain anyway. He made a face at the discomfort. The crackers and cheese in his mouth threatened to choke him.

11

"Gawdamn, we got us a real Chinatown going up here," Lucy said with her hands on her hips as she studied all the activity.

"Yeah, honey, we got them working, ain't we," Burns said with his arm over her shoulder. Their small tents were in a row, and the workers scurried around using wheelbarrows. The sound of picking and shoveling came from the shaft. Busy as beavers, they were. Burns felt smug about his mining operation.

The next thing he needed was some wagons to haul the ore and a sluice at Owl Creek to wash it in the creek. He had found several pinhead nuggets in the ore they'd brought him. In a short while, he would be sporting around San Francisco with Lucy on his arm and folks saying things like: "Isn't that the gold baron of Arizona?"

He needed a better foreman than that rat-faced Frenchman Default. If the Chinese weren't such good workers, he would have had to boss them himself. He'd speak to Mick about someone else doing the job instead of Default.

"They finding anything worthwhile?" Lucy asked, breaking his thoughts.

"Plenty of color. I've checked several samples. We can wash the loose stuff in a sluice and get lots of gold out of it."

"Down in the creek, huh?"

"Yeah, but that's no problem. We'll hire a few teamsters to haul the ore, and I'll move half this bunch down there to wash it. Look here." He held up a small nugget that shined in the sun. "See there. I found it just dry-panning with my hand this morning."

"How much are them Chinks stealing from you?" she asked under her breath. She nodded in their direction as the wind swept her duster open. Then she quickly closed it so none of them could see her white legs.

"They steal any, they're dead."

"Ha, them slant-eyed bastards are probably hiding your nuggets away like a squirrel does nuts."

"I catch one doing it, I'll cut his throat."

"Suit yourself, but they are stealing from you."

"How do you know so much about them stealing?"

"I was raised in California. Everyone there knows how they steal."

"I'll keep an eye out for that. The biggest thing is getting a stamping mill set up to break up the rock so we can get the gold out of that. That will cost lots of money."

"If you make enough out of the loose gold, you can buy one," she said flippantly. He realized she had no idea of the amount of money required for a stamper operation.

Mines required investors from places like New York, San Francisco—hell, even St. Louis, if you could find one there with enough money. He'd probably have to issue stocks to raise enough capital—maybe on that Mountain Board of Trade in Denver.

"That sluicing business in the creek won't go fast enough," he said to her. Women simply did not understand about business. Oh, well, she could do other things quite well. He reached down and patted her butt.

His action drew a sleepy-eyed suggestive look from her.

Lucy was always in heat. Before he went back inside with her, he had to speak to Default, maybe send him to Owl Creek to get Mick up here. This mining operation was fast taking on more importance than the saloon, as far as he was concerned. They had a real good deal if they could get it all working.

"Go back to the cabin. I'm going to find that Frenchman and send him after Mick. I need some things done, and faster than they are happening right now."

"I'll be there—waiting for you," she said, and batted her long lashes at him, letting her fingers trail down his sleeve.

"Good," he said, and set out looking for the man.

He found him sitting on a log near the shaft, obviously hung over again.

"Default, who is in charge among these men?"

"That man over there. Name is Two something." Default pointed to a small man busy giving orders in a whiny Chinese accent.

"He speak English?"

"Yeah, some, why?"

"I want you to ride to Owl Creek and get Mick up here. While you're gone, I wanted to know the boss of them so I can tell them what to do."

"Yeah, Two, he's the one." Default dropped his head and closed his eyes as if in pain.

"Good, you go get Mick. He's long overdue up here."

"You're the boss," Default said and rose to his feet. "Two! Come meet the boss." He waved the little man over.

Two stood maybe five feet tall. His queue hung down his back, and his small mustache was twisted in a thin string on both sides of his mouth. He bowed when he arrived.

"This is the boss," Default said.

"Nice to meet you, Boss."

"You get fifty cents more a day," Burns said to the man. "For being such a good foreman."

"Thanks you, bossie man." The man bowed again.

"Default is going to Owl Creek on business, so if you need anything, then you come get me. Understand?"

"Oh, yes. We all work hard." He extended his small hands toward the men.

"Yes, you keep working. There will be a big bonus for all the men." Burns had no intention of touching a gaw-damn Chinese or shaking his hand. Why, they might have some kind of disease. Weird people—and what the hell would a handshake mean to them anyway?

"Thank you. Thank you." Two bowed again, and then when Burns indicated he could go back, he hurried to the hole and shouted something in Chinese to the others. They all went: "Ah!"

Burns felt convinced he was on the right track with these Chinks. Default gave him a small wave and walked off. Burns hoped the man was going to find a horse and ride for Owl Creek. He neither trusted the man nor considered him dependable. But obviously Mick did. And the Irishman had more experience with the likes of such thugs to know one who was loyal and tough—two attributes that made a man like Default valuable, despite his lack of ambition and listlessness. And that could be attributed to his obvious ad-diction to the bottle. Burns decided to go back to the cabin and idle some time away with Lucy while he waited for Flannery's arrival.

Back in Owl Creek, Flannery had taken a spot on the saloon porch in the warming sun. The pain in his rib cage had let up, but the heartburn from his eating was growing. Over-head, the carpenters were nailing on the shingles. He could see that they were unloading wagons of furniture down the road at the Silver King.

What had he heard? In two days they planned to be open with a free barbeque of two elks, several deer, and bear meat and four free kegs of beer. They'd start off with a bang—he wanted to meet the man who was going to run it. Word was out some rich men in Prescott had footed the bill for the place and they'd hired a professional to operate it.

No matter how hard Flannery tried to find out the backers' names, they were still unknown, as was the name of the gent who was going to manage it. Flannery hated a mystery worse than anything else, especially one that could affect him.

The Arnold woman had hired some young boys to help her in the restaurant, and had offered a reward for the Chinese girl's return. He grinned to himself. If she knew that bitch was in his shack, what would she do? Probably send a bunch of her customers up to storm his place. It made him angry just thinking about her getting off without paying him. Still, he felt she was too damn powerful for him to mess with until he had enough men on his payroll to spread fear among the miners.

That day would come. He pounded the discomfort in his chest with his fist and wished it would go away. It had come more often the past month. Must be the altitude hurting him. It hadn't been this bad in Yuma, but the damn heat had cooked his brain there.

"Hey, the manager of the Silver King's coming tomorrow," a passing miner said to him.

"Yeah, what's his name?"

"I ain't heard that. Only that he's coming." The man strode on toward the Arnold woman's tent. Flannery made a face at his back. No one knew a gawdamn thing. It really pissed him off. The fact that Slocum was not dead didn't help. Like a shot, he bent over in pain as if struck by lightning. He pulled his shoulders together, and then closed his eyes as more knives ran down his arms. What was happening?

12

Slocum sat up in the high-back rocker. His right arm was in a sling, and he still felt depleted, but some of his strength had returned. He had not taken any of the medicine since the night before. Better to wean himself off that stuff—it made him crazy. The shoulder hurt a lot, actually throbbed, but he could stand the pain. If the shooter came back, he wanted to be certain he could handle himself well enough to survive.

"You look much better today," Mae said with a smile as she came through the front door of the doctor's house with a rustle of her stiff dress. "Is that Arnold woman coming to take you back to Owl Creek today?"

"I don't think so. I asked for her to wait a couple of days so I could get stronger."

"She's kinda got her cap set for you, hasn't she?"

"I guess." He hadn't considered much about their relationship since the shooting and all of his wild dreams on the laudanum.

"Slocum, I know you. You don't ever guess about anything. I'd say unless you turn tail and run soon, she's planning permanent things for the two of you."

"She tell you so?" he asked, thinking over the notion. He could do a lot worse than settle down somewhere with Hap Arnold.

"Tell me so? No, she didn't need to tell me one thing." Mae shook her head in disapproval. "But I know women, and that one is dead set on having you."

They both laughed.

"What else do you know?" he asked to change the subject.

"I know all about this fella they hired to run the Silver King Saloon up there. He's coming up."

"Who's that?"

"He comes from New Mexico. I've never heard of him before. Buster Markley is his name." She went to the front window and looked out with her back turned toward him. "He's supposed to know how to run one."

"He does." Slocum suddenly felt better, knowing that his old partner was coming to him. Markley would soon be in his grasp.

"You know him?" She whirled and gave him a questioning look.

"Yes, and he owes me money." Slocum drew a breath.

"Very much?"

"Oh, enough. But thanks for the information. Where did you learn that?"

"Laying on my back, where else?" She frowned at him.

"I meant, who told you?"

"Some man from Prescott who came up to check on his mining operation. He wants me to go up there to Owl Creek and go to work for Markley. Said that when he came up each week, he and I, well, you know, we could tussle on the sheets. I think he must like me." A sly smile crossed her lips.

"You're easy to like, Mae," Slocum said. "What's his name?"

"The man from Prescott?"

"Yes."

"Thomas Goldring the Third."

Slocum shook his head. He didn't know the man, but he sounded important—*the Third*.

"Oh, he has a fat little wife that doesn't like to do it. You must know the story—it's the same old story all those kinds of men tell all us doves. How she just lays on her back when he's got it in her and won't wiggle a little finger." She shook her head in disbelief. "What the hell did they marry them for?"

"Prestige?"

"Yeah, that's it. Damn sure wasn't for pleasure, to hear them talk." She wrinkled her nose and turned back to stare out the window.

"You going up there to Owl Creek?" he asked.

"I might. What kind of a man is Markley? Can he stand up to Flannery?"

"I think so."

"Then I may go. I'm tired of this place. And this Goldring ain't bad. I mean, I know he only wants to use my ass. I'm not stupid. But a gal can use some of that pretend tenderness in a world of bathless, rutting males wanting to just stick it in her all the time."

"I understand," he said, wanting to show his concern for her. So Markley was coming to Owl Creek. Why all the secrecy? Did the man know Slocum was looking up there for him? Probably not. Slocum hadn't even checked on him being in Prescott, he'd been so concerned about recovering his dun horse. Time would tell. Slocum tried to push his back into the chair and force some of the pain out of his body. One thing for certain, he would have to be better than this and a lot stronger to ever confront his ex-partner. A lot stronger.

Mick Flannery blinked when he saw Default coming up the valley all slouched in the saddle on the Indian pony. He checked the sun—it was near noon. What was wrong at the mine? He had been checking on things at the bar on the porch. Earlier he'd sent Evers home for some rest so he could work as bartender later on. No one was about, and Flannery could stand guard until he ordered the Kid out of the shack to take his place. He'd give him a little more time to feel sorry for himself. Then he would kick him in the ass and make him guard things. What's going on?'' he demanded as the Frenchman reined up.

''He wants to see you up there.'' Default dropped from the saddle and then bent over and rubbed his knees as if they were hurting him.

''How's it going up there?''

''Them Chinks is working.''

''What's wrong then?''

''He wants to see you. Burns wants to see you.''

''What for?''

''Christ, I don't know. He's such a gawdamn big man. Hell, he speaks to me like I'm one of them damn Chinamen.''

''He's got class.''

''He can stick that up his ass.'' Default shook his head as if he didn't give a damn. Then a twinkle shone in his beady eyes. ''But I'd like to have *her*, though.''

''Yeah, Lucy.'' Then Flannery recalled the China girl in the shack. Lucy would bitch that he hadn't taken her up there. Let her bitch.

''Anything wrong up there?'' Flannery repeated.

''No, he wants to see you. Said you needed to send some wagons up and get the washer ready.''

Flannery considered the new mission. He had done nothing about the washer, nor the teams. Hell, he was only one man. He tried to recall the man who was wanting to sell his claim in the creek—he had heard something about it in the bar the night before. He'd better check on that.

Maybe Kramer's freighters would haul down the ore. No, they were lumber haulers. It took mule skinners to haul ore. Maybe he should go to Prescott and find out where they were at. First, he better buy that claim in the creek so they had a place to work it.

"What you want me to do?" Default asked, wiping his lips on the back of his hand like a man dying for a drink.

"I guess you need to go into Prescott and hire some ore wagons."

"All the way back there?"

"Dammit, I've got a bar to run, a claim to buy, and then go up there and satisfy him. Which one of those you want to do?"

"You got a bottle?"

"I've got a pint. But you better get those ore haulers and get back here in two days."

"I ain't failed you yet. What's the Kid doing?"

"He ran into a blackjack."

"Huh?" Default blinked his eyes. "Whose blackjack?"

"Mine, for disobeying my orders." Flannery went, found him a pint of whiskey from a box behind the bar, and returned. "You get those wagons and get right back."

"How many?" Default asked as he took the bottle and looked at the label.

"Not less than two."

"What if—"

"Gawdammit, hire them!"

"Mick, you're getting awful red-faced," Default said, concerned.

Short of breath, Flannery dropped to his butt on the edge of the porch. His heart was running away again. It thundered in his chest cavity, and he couldn't get enough air. This damn elevation was going to be the death of him yet.

"You all right, Mick?"

"Yeah, fine, I've got indigestion is all. Damn crackers and cheese does that to me at times." He slowly recovered, and then he stood up for show.

"Yeah, they do that to me too. I'm going to Prescott?" Default waited for Flannery's final words.

"Go. Get the wagons. Is there gold up there?" he asked under his breath.

"I think so. Lots of pinhead nuggets in the tailings."

"Good," Flannery said despite the lead weight in his chest. "Maybe we'll all get rich yet."

When Default was on his way, Flannery hurried off to locate the man ready to sell his claim in the creek. He recalled his name was Swenson. He strode along the rushing creek, listening to the ring of metal shovels and gravel as men labored to fill their sluices.

"Swenson," he shouted above the stream's rush, and a tall lanky man under a floppy-brimmed wool felt hat rose up. Flannery waved him over as he considered how the claims were laid. The road was high up on this side, and the wagons would have to cross lower down and bring the ore up on the other side. Plenty of muddy water swept past, and with a little damming, he could have a larger sluice in place in no time at all.

"This your claim?" Flannery asked as the man waded closer and leaned on his long-handled shovel.

"Sure is. From those stakes up there to those down there, she's my claim. Why? You want to buy it?"

"If I can afford it." Mick had seen the markers. Eventually, if this worked out, he would need three more claims for their operation, but Swenson's would do for the time being.

"Oh, I'd sell it cheap. Getting lots of color. I've washed up a couple ounces a week here."

"What do you want for it?" Mick didn't give a damn about a two-ounce-a-week find. They needed a real big run for their operation. Like twenty or more ounces per hour.

"What do you want for it?" Flannery asked him again.

"A thousand dollars." The Swede beamed as if he was serious.

What the hell did he think he had, the gawdamn mother lode? Stupid bastard, asking a thousand dollars for thirty feet of stream. Why, you could buy a block in San Francisco for that price.

"Five hundred," Flannery offered.

"No, I'll make more than that in a couple months washing this gravel right here."

"Seven-fifty, and that's my final offer." The stupid bastard better take it, if he knew what was good for him.

"You going to work it yourself?" The man leaned his long chin over his shovel handle and then rested it on top of it.

"I have workers." Was he going to take the offer or not?

"I guess I'll sell it," he said slowly and then continued, talking his plans out loud. "I sure hate to sell that cheap, but I got a wife back in Kansas and we've got a farm. That much money will pay off the mortgage, and the gold dust I've got saved will buy teams, seed, and new farm machinery. You know they got wheat reapers now?"

"I heard that. Come up to the saloon to sign the papers and I'll pay you," Flannery said as he considered the dumb farmer. You damn stupid Swede. You ain't getting away from the Bradshaws with the money I pay you. It sure won't go to pay for no dirt farm or damn reaper machine. I'll have all of it back before you get to Iron Mountain, and your gold dust as well.

"Boys," Swenson shouted as he waded out in his hip gum boots, "I'm selling out."

The three men downstream waved at him.

"You ain't leaving already, are you?" one asked with a hint of disappointment.

"Yeah, Katy is waiting for me." A grin spread over his red face as he considered his wife in Kansas. "I get my boots off and my things gathered, I'll be coming after my money," he said to Flannery.

"I'll be waiting." With that Flannery turned and started back.

He headed upstream, satisfied the man would come along

in a short while to the saloon. Then he would have to follow him and get the money back. There was that much cash in the saloon bank, and Burns wanted a claim on the creek to wash his ore in. So all Mick had to do was knock Swenson in the head on the road somewhere, and he'd be seven-fifty richer, not counting the man's gold dust. The plan sounded fine.

Upstream, he crossed the creek on the log bridge and went toward the saloon. He could hear the crack of hammers. Those lazy carpenters should finish the roof shingles by dark, and he could move everything inside in a day. He could hardly believe it. They still lacked finishing lots on the inside, but they'd soon have a saloon to do business in.

Maybe he'd throw a free barbeque of his own and compete with the Silver King's big plans. That new man was coming—he'd heard the rumors. He still didn't know his name, probably never heard of him anyway. They'd for sure hire some hardcase. But no matter. This was Mick's camp to work, and he'd cross that bridge when he got to it. He'd sent Default for the ore wagons, and now he was about to get Swenson's claim. He paused to catch his breath. If Burns didn't like it, he could come do some work himself.

His heart was running away again. He could feel it under his palm, which was pressed hard to his rib cage, pounding like a racehorse's hooves inside there. Damn this high country anyway.

13

The afternoon sun hung above the treetops. Slocum had used up most of his newfound energy walking out on the ridge that stretched behind the doc's small house. His sore shoulder still throbbed with pulsating pain. On his stroll to test his strength, he had handled the Colt in his left hand, felt the heft, and taken aim with it several times. He knew he could fire it with his left fist, but he wouldn't be as fast or as accurate as with his right one. That was the price he had to pay. He seated himself on a log and tried to clear his head.

If Flannery had been the shooter, he must know by this time that he had failed. When would he come back to try again? How could Slocum prove it had been Flannery? All good questions that needed an answer. Answers that all evaded him stranded at the doc's place, miles from Owl Creek. Even Mae had learned more than he could; he had no real proof about the gunman's idenity. He had worn a bowler. So did many others. It could have been Markley as well—he usually wore a bowler.

Slocum rose and headed back for the house. There was too much that he didn't know about this deal, and one thing for certain—his shoulder would not heal fast enough to suit him.

"You must be getting stronger," Doc Halpin said as Slocum entered the house. The medium-built man, with his bushy hair in its usual windswept style and his clean-shaven face, was washing his hands.

"Yes, some," Slocum said as he watched the man finish washing his hands and then dry them on a Turkish towel. "How is the patient you went to check on?" he asked the physician.

"Dead."

"Oh."

"Not much you can do for lockjaw. He must have had that iron nail in the frog of his hoof for weeks. I burned it out with turpentine, but it had been too infected by the time the man called me. Good draft animal. I hated to lose him."

"Much difference between horses and people?" Slocum asked.

"Yeah, horses can't tell you where they hurt."

Both men laughed.

"I'm having a stiff shot of whiskey. You want one?" Doc asked.

"Never turn down good liquor."

"I guess there is no end to bloodshed in this country," Doc said, taking down the bottle. "They found another man murdered on the Prescott road. Took his body in to the sheriff, but that man won't even ride out here to check on things. Guess it won't do any good. He couldn't find out anything anyway."

"Who was it?"

"Some miner with his pockets lined with dust. Enough for someone to hit him in the head for it. Even if he didn't have two ounces." Doc came beside Slocum as he looked out at the street. Four men rode by on the road. Under bowlers and in brown plaid suits, they wore long mustaches and rode with the stiffness of men more used to a dealer's chair than a saddle. It was the man in the center that Slocum noticed, fuller-faced and his eyes more almond-shaped at the corners. Buster Markley and his saloon crew were on their way to Owl Creek. He went in tough enough company these days.

Why shouldn't he? Someone else was paying for them. Slocum thought for a minute the second man on the far side was Ed Snead, but he couldn't be certain. Ed had dealt faro in Silver City. He soon looked at their backs.

"You know them?" Doc asked.

"One was my ex-partner who ran out on me with my money." Slocum turned around, still uncertain how he would face that bunch. He would have to separate them to get to Buster. That would be no easy task. He accepted the glass of amber liquor from Doc.

"To your better health," Doc said, and they clinked glasses in agreement.

And soon, Slocum added to himself.

Flannery had Swenson sign the claim form that he had drawn up. It all looked legal enough, and he paid the man as they stood at the new bar. The thud of hammers rang all around them, and the sweet smell of sawdust filled the saloon.

"How about a drink to celebrate?" Flannery did not want to sound too anxious. He had devised a plan to save him from having to chase this Swede down. Gabe was in on it, though he did not know the extent of the man's new-found wealth.

"I guess one; this is the biggest sum of money I ever had in my life," Swenson said carefully, stuffing the bills in a drawstring purse and then shoving it down in his front pants pocket. The hump of it looked out of place, to the side of where men usually bulged out their pants.

"Gabe, pour our man a good drink."

"Oh, I just wanted a beer," Swenson protested.

"A beer to seal a deal of this size? Unheard of. Try some real whiskey. Why, in a few years you will be the biggest farmer in northern Kansas, and only the best whiskey will be poured in your glass to salute you.''

Swenson grinned like a store-window cat. Flannery knew he had struck a real vein with the stupid Swede. Gabe had poured the double-strong whiskey for his man. They had laid their plans out ahead of time; if they only could trick Swenson into drinking it. Flannery felt a shiver of excitement at the sight of the man taking his first gulp of the liquor.

"Whew!" Swenson said in a gasp. "This is real strong stuff, huh?"

"Cuts the dust, don't it?" Flannery said, and then downed his. "Not bad stuff, is it?"

"Kinda powerful stuff," the Swede said, looking at the glass in doubt.

"You'll get use to it," Flannery promised with his hand on the man's big bony shoulder.

"I guess I will."

Coaxing and talking, he soon had Swenson well on his way to drinking his second glass. He shared a secret puzzled look with Gabe. Few men ever lasted more than one glass of the 180-proof mixed in a little tea for coloring. The big man was halfway into the second one when he looked at them dazed and then his knees collapsed.

Flannery rushed in to catch him.

"My gosh, Gabe. Swenson must have fainted. Help get him to my shack to sleep it off."

They managed to get underneath the man's arms and support him as he began to mumble about Kate. Oh, his Kate! When they reached the shack with him, the Kid opened the door.

"We can get him from here," Flannery said to the bartender. The man didn't need to know anything about the Chink being in there, or about the money they planned to remove from Swenson's person.

"Get under Swenson's arm and help me get him inside," Flannery said to the Kid.

"Say, thanks, Gabe," Flannery added, and then he and the Kid staggered under the bigger man's weight. By this time, Swenson was past mumbling anything sensible. "We've got him. You go back and watch the bar."

'Sure, Boss."

"We're fine," Flannery said, concerned that Gabe might spot the girl.

"See you two later," Gabe said, and to Flannery's relief the man hurried off.

"What we doing with him?" the Kid asked as they went through the doorway.

"He's going to have an accident," Flannery said under his breath as he kicked the door shut behind them. "I bought his claim, and he ain't leaving town that rich."

"He have a rich claim?" the Kid asked after they dumped Swenson on the cot.

"No, but he had one in the creek that we need to wash the ore from the shaft."

"I don't understand."

"You don't have to," Flannery said, and placed a feather pillow over the man's face. He pressed down hard on both sides.

"Hold his arms," he said to the Kid. "He may fight this."

Swenson's body tried to roll away as the seconds ticked away. Flannery pressed harder and harder, his strength winning the battle. The Kid fought with his arms, and then Swenson in a great effort arched his back, and at last fell limp. Flannery held the pillow down longer for a slow count of thirty, then stood up. His chest hurt, and he staggered aside.

Half braced on the table, he searched the room. An explosion inside his rib cage was drumming like bolts of cannon fire to his brain, and his left arm ached to the fingers. The worst spell yet. He stared in a stupor at the pale-faced Swede as he raged for his breath. At least that son of a bitch was dead.

"Where's that girl?" he asked, not seeing her in the room.

The Kid whirled around and blinked in disbelief. "Where did she go? Honest, she was here a minute ago. I swear she was here. Dammit, Flannery, you've got to believe me!"

"Find her. She talks and we're dead men."

"I will." And the Kid rushed outside without his hat.

Flannery fought for control of his breathing, dizzy-headed and shaken from the exertion. His damn heart was still kicking him like a mule. Maybe he should take the money he got off Swenson, the saloon bank money, and what he had collected from Kramer and and leave these damn mountains. He had to do something and do it soon. But if they didn't catch that China girl before she talked to the others, he'd probably not live long anyway. She knew enough to tell a miners court, or any court for that matter.

He'd better go help the Kid find her. Damn things got so damn involved in no time at all. All he wanted to do was recover the money, and she'd gone and run off. No justice in this world for him.

14

"Slocum, wake up. Wake up!"

"What is it?" he asked, blinking at the light from the lamp she held in her hand. She swung it aside and he looked squarely into the serious expression on Hap Arnold's face.

"What's happening?" he asked as the bolt of pain shot from his shoulder, reminding him of the wound.

"Lou Wee saw Flannery smother a man to death tonight up at his shack."

"Who?" He decided that she had seen his underwear before, so he sat up with some discomfort and threw his legs over the side of the bed.

"We need to send for the sheriff," Doc said, joining them. "This killing has gone far enough."

"But he won't come up here," she said in disgust. "There's been enough killings at Owl Creek reported to him, not to mention the ones here at Iron Mountain. He never does anything if he does come out. He gets his votes in Prescott and from some of those big ranchers. Why, most of these miners can't read or write, and damn sure don't vote, and chances are they won't even be in his county when the next election rolls around."

"We should let the law handle it." Slocum rubbed the back of his neck, trying to think the thing out.

"The law will," she said. "They're wanting a miners court up at Owl Creek. Folks all think that you should ramrod it."

"That's illegal where they have laws, Hap." He frowned at her suggestion.

"We don't have any laws at all in the Bradshaws, and until we do, we need to get rid of the riffraff like Flannery."

"I'm not in any shape—"

"They know that. They'll bring them in and then give them a fair trial. They want you to be the judge."

"But I'm not a judge," he said.

"Yes, you are. They elected you to that job."

He shook his head. "Because I wasn't there?"

"No, because you stood up to Flannery and the Kid."

"So we tell them to leave Owl Creek and what then?"

"No, the miners want them tried for murdering Swenson first."

"Doc, I guess I have no choice but to go see about it. How much do I owe you?"

Doc dismissed it with a wave of his hand. "Nothing. You're good company. You have any problems with that shoulder, you get here in a hurry. You were lucky that cheap bullet of his was loaded light, or you'd have had a hole in your shoulder big enough to drive a wagon through you. Take care now."

"Turn your head," Slocum said to Hap as he prepared to rise. "I'll dress."

"You'll need some help," she said, holding out his pants.

"Fine," he agreed.

"Where is the Chinese girl at?" he asked, putting one foot in a leg of the britches.

"In hiding. Where they won't find her." Hap shook her head. "They kept her naked up there."

"Since she's the only witness to the murder, I hope she's safe." He stepped into the other leg, and Hap pulled the pants up around his waist.

"She's safe, trust me. I guess you'll wear that sling under your shirt?" She finished buttoning his fly for him, and then gave the waistband a jerk upward that forced him on his toes.

"I will," he said, shaking his head in disapproval at her actions.

"I'm hoping the ride doesn't shake you up too bad. But we figured I'd draw less attention coming after you than several men leaving camp." She held out his shirt for his good arm, and then she wrapped it around him.

Like a mother hen, she buttoned up the front of the shirt, and then shoved it in his pants with a wink as she stood on her toes to do it. In the close proximity to her, he could smell food odors in her hair, mainly tangy cinnamon from her pies, but most of all he could smell the honey-like musk of her body. Another time, another place—for him, perhaps, another life would be necessary, since he had already messed this one up so bad—and they would have made a great team.

He thanked the doc again, and then he and Hap hurried out and climbed in the waiting wagon. A quarter moon hung over the pines, and she made the team hurry through the inky night. There were patches of gray ground in the open, and the darkness swallowed them when they passed under the groves of ponderosas.

The clop of the team and the creak of the wagon rims filled the night. They occasionally scraped a rock surface that made the wheels ring. His good shoulder rubbed hers as she drove with purpose, using all the visibility they had to hurry.

They emerged from the cavern-like darkness of the trees into the moonlight again. Then they began the descent down the narrow long passage that clung to the side of the mountain and took them eventually down into Owl Creek. There were hundreds of feet of sheer granite to the side and above them on the stone face of the mountain.

"Pretty country," he said under his breath as if someone might hear them.

"It is in the daytime. I'm getting so I don't even mind it," she said, her knuckles white under the starlight as she gripped the reins.

"The miners say that this fancy dude Burns moved in and has a dozen Chinese working the McRoy claim," she offered.

"You know him, this Burns?" he asked.

"We thought he was backing Flannery's saloon, but him and some fallen angel called Lucy are living in McRoy's log cabin."

"And?"

"The miners court wants to know how he got that claim."

"Did they ask him?"

"No, but you can."

"They're leaving lots for me to do."

"Exactly."

He reached for his sore shoulder. It hurt, but he would make the run. She swerved the team aside, and he had to catch his balance. "Are you going to make it?" She glanced over at him.

"If you don't drive too close to that edge I will." He indicated the side by the bluff. "Drive over there, please."

"Had to miss that boulder in the road, or I'd have spilled you over anyway."

"Good. Stay as close to that wall as you can. There's a lot of empty space out there that I don't intend to fill up."

"I'm doing the best that I can."

"You're doing wonderful, Hap. Just stay away from that edge." He raised his gaze to the stars for help.

"I can't find her," the Kid said, out of breath. "I've been everywhere. I tore that Arnold woman's stuff apart. She ain't there either."

"Where was she staying before then?"

"I don't know. She was hanging around camp is all I know."

"We don't find her, we better get out of here."

"Who's going to do anything? I need some sleep."

"Them miners will hang us if she ever talks about us killing Swenson."

"Them miners ain't nothing," the Kid scoffed.

"Them miners can be a lynch mob, and I've seen them mobs before." Flannery felt struck down by the very notion. Just talk of a miners court put fear in any gambler's or saloon keeper's soul. Such courts handled things like lightning, and they weren't real fussy how they did it. He'd seen two gamblers who'd had cards up their sleeves when they were arrested, and they'd been hung from a wagon yard cross post right outside the court.

He'd even seen a man hung for feeding the camp dog meat in its stew. Another was hung for beating his girl-friend with a cane when she tried to hold back some of her whoring money from him. They treated murderers and thieves alike—no, he wouldn't be there for any miners court trial. Not if he could help it.

He suddenly caught the Kid by the sleeve and held him back in the light glow of dawn. They were a hundred feet from the shack, and he could see the door was open and four men were carrying Swenson out. Too late! Damn, oh, damn.

"They've got Swenson," the Kid hissed.

"I can see that," he said, dragging the Kid further back into the shadows.

"What'll we do?"

"When they get gone," he said under his breath, "and if they ain't left no guards behind, we've got to get our horses and get out of here before daylight."

"Ain't we tough enough?" The two of them crouched behind packing crates stacked in a pile, trying to see if there was any sign of a guard.

"We ain't shit—listen to me. Our time is up here. If you don't want to hang, then you better follow me real close."

"I sure don't want to hang."

"Come on then, they're gone." Flannery started out at a crouch, running to the corral. His heart hurt him as he hurriedly saddled his horse with trembling fingers. His breath was gone when he finished cinching him up. He mounted with great effort, and the two of them tore out of camp. Flannery clung to the saddle horn, unable to even get his breath, and wondering if he could hang on long enough to get away. He was close on the Kid's paint's heels.

Once they were out of camp and down the valley, he reined up. He turned to listen. No sounds of pursuit—good, maybe they had escaped clean. They needed to warn Burns next. He would be furious, but there was nothing they could do about that. They could not use the Prescott road as a route out—the miners would cover it. They'd have to cross the mountains to the east somehow to get over to the Black Canyon road. It would take them down to Phoenix, and they could catch a stage from there for the train. Maybe even go up to Globe, where the big copper strike was and where no one knew them.

He fought for his breath. No time to lose. He grimaced in pain, then booted his horse after the Kid.

They reached the McRoy claim in the early dawn. The Kid got off and pounded on the door.

"Yeah, yeah, this better be good," Burns said inside, pulling on his pants. "What the hell's going on?" he roared, opening the door with a Colt in his fist.

He looked out as the Kid backed up, and then he spotted Flannery, pale as a ghost, clinging to his saddlehorn and trying to stand beside his horse. "What is this?" Burns demanded.

"They found Swenson and that Chinese girl run off," the Kid babbled.

"Make sense, man!"

"We got Swenson to sign his claim in the creek over to you," Flannery explained, then tried to recover his breath at the same time. "Then we killed him to get your money back."

"That damn Chinese bitch run out and told them," the Kid said, leaning his back against the log wall, too tired to stand on his own.

"Ah, hell," Flannery said beside himself with the pain. "We looked all night for her. Then they come got his body out of the shack. We knew they—"

"What about my investment?" Burns demanded.

"Hell, you can face a miners court. I ain't going to be here for it."

"I'm sure they'd listen to reason," Burns said. He shook his head to dismiss their concern. "It's your word versus some hysterical Chinese whore."

"You don't know miners courts, Burns."

"He's right, darling," Lucy said as she wrapped the red duster around her. "I've seen them before in action. They ain't like your regular court. They hang you and boom, it is all over."

"I've invested thousands," he protested, and shook his head in disbelief.

"If these men are leaving," she said, "then I am going with them. I won't be here for them to get me on the stand. No, sir, I'm leaving."

"I haven't done a damn thing but work a claim since I got here," Burns said. "I'm not leaving all of this because some damned old miners think they can bluff me. Flannery, you and the Kid stay here with me. We can hold them off."

"Saddle me a horse, Kid," Lucy said. "Burns, you ain't never seen these courts in action." Then she ran inside the cabin.

Burns stormed in after her. "You ain't taking any of that jewelry if you're running out on me."

"Screw the jewelry, my life is worth more than that."

"You ain't leaving!" he shouted, and then he twisted her around by the arms.

"Let go of me!" she said, coldly enough that he obeyed her.

The hell with her. He could find all kinds of women. Whores were a cheap commodity. He could get another. Besides, *she'd* made the fuss about getting that Chinese bitch back, which had caused all his troubles in the first place.

Flannery could run, Burns figured. But they wouldn't get *him*. He was tougher than some grubby miners anyway. Let them come, and he'd hold an army off by himself if it was necessary.

She filled a pillowcase with things, and then dressed in her divided riding skirt. She stalked outside without a word to him. Some gratitude for him putting up with her all this time. The bitch.

"We've all got to go," the Kid said almost apologetically as he helped Lucy into the saddle. "They're going to hang us."

"I ain't done nothing wrong," Burns snapped as he watched them ride off. "You all are cowards!" he shouted after them.

Then he dried his hands on his pants. What about his saloon and the money and the supplies? Maybe he'd better hire him some guns. No, he could handle matters. He'd been in worse scrapes than this, and had handled all of them. Let them mess with him, they'd learn a thing or two.

From his vantage point at the edge of the grove that sheltered the cabin, he could see her red hair flaming in the first light of dawn as they rode up the side of the canyon headed east. Going to Crown King, he guessed—it was somewhere over there. Ride away, you stinking whore! I'll find better than you anywhere. Cheap bitch—run at the first word of danger! And Flannery, that worthless Irish bastard, he deserved that whiny pimple-faced Kid—he could have him clear to Hell.

He gawdamn sure wasn't giving up on a million-dollar strike—there were tons of gold in this mine. He could see it every day in the ore they brought up. He had the mother lode, and they were riding out on the chance of a lifetime.

"I hope you fall out of the saddle and break your damn necks!" he screamed after them, and then stomped his bare foot in anger. Stomped it so hard he limped as he went back to the cabin to make plans.

15

"This is a miners' court hearing," Christianson, the prosecutor, said as he paced around the saloon, appropriated for the purpose of holding trials. He was a short man, his brown hair parted in the center and his face clean-shaven, and he looked every bit the role he played. Behind him sat a room full of grim-faced men, many bearded and still coated with dust and mud from their work.

"His Honor Judge Slocum will preside."

"Yes," came the chorus of approval. The various men nodded and spoke approvingly of his appointment in low voices.

"First the untimely death of Charlie McRoy will be examined," the prosecutor said. He was dressed in a checkered suit that had been taken out of a trunk and still bore many of the wrinkles from its trip there, but despite his short size, he looked very tall swaggering around in the area before where Slocum sat behind the bench, which was draped with black cloth. "If that pleases the court?"

"It does," Slocum said with a nod. It would be a long day. But after many hours of discussion with Christianson and the other leaders of the camp, the plans had been laid for the sessions.

"Can we also ask that four men go bring Mick Flannery and the Val Verde Kid back here to answer questions of this court concerning the murder of Olaf Swenson?"

A murmur of "yes" went up from the crowd, and Slocum used the gavel to silence the talking. "He needs four volunteers to bring them back."

"Where did they go?" one bearded man asked, standing behind the rail fencing.

"They ran off," someone hissed impatiently at him.

"Oh, I see," he said, and sat down, drawing laughter from his cohorts.

"Four men?" the prosecutor asked again. "I need four volunteers."

They began to file forward.

"Do all of you have horses to use?" Slocum asked the men.

"I don't," the man on the end said.

"You may use my dun," Slocum told the miner.

"Should we bring them back alive?" one man asked.

"We prefer they come back alive," Slocum said. "And stand trial."

"Yes."

"I'll go with them," the hunter Duggan said, pushing his way through the crowd. "I know the ways of these mountains better than any man."

"Yes!" came the shout of approval.

"Very good. Raise your right hands," Slocum said, and swore them in as enforcers of the court. Then he turned to the fiery prosecutor. "Let us begin the hearings on the death of Charlie McRoy."

Slocum leaned back in the barrel-backed wooden chair with some discomfort. Owl Creek Miners Court was in session. It was almost funny when Markley walked in, looked up, and saw him for the first time seated behind the bench. His face went pale. Slocum's new position would obviously cause his ex-partner considerable discomfort this day.

Christianson called the first witness to the stand.

"You knew the deceased Charles McRoy?" he asked.

"Yes, and I was the one found him shot," the man said.

"Did McRoy say anything to you?"

"He said, 'They got me, boys.' That was all."

"He never said who got him?"

"No, sir."

The testimony went on for hours, but no revelation came forth, and Slocum found that the pain increased in his shoulder as each hour ticked away. At last, he rapped the gavel at a convenient break. "Court adjourned until further notice," he said with another rap of the gavel.

Christianson rushed over and looked upset.

"We aren't going to continue?"

"I can't see the point. There is nothing to implicate anyone in the shooting. You need a witness or evidence or something. To talk all day and prove nothing will wear the miners out and they will lose faith in their own system," Slocum said under his breath.

"Then let's start the hearing on Swenson's murder tomorrow. We have a good eyewitness for it."

Slocum nodded as if taking the matter under consideration. "Christianson, you can't get a conviction on the testimony of a Chinese girl alone."

"I have witnesses that found the body all blue-faced in Flannery's shack."

"That's good. Do you have any other evidence?"

"Yes. Swenson sold his claim to a Harvey Burns for seven-fifty, and there was no money on the body, so he obviously was robbed. The purpose of the murder."

"Then he did not sell it to Flannery?" Slocum asked, considering the news.

"No, he sold it to Burns. I guess Flannery worked for him."

"Burns is the man on McRoy's claim now?"

"Yes. He has it crawling with Chinese, they say."

"So perhaps he could explain how he got that claim to

a jury?'' Slocum nodded to himself at the notion. He had almost forgotten his throbbing shoulder.

"I knew you'd figure out something." Christianson smiled, pleased with Slocum. "Should I have Burns brought in?''

"Is he still up there or did he leave with Flannery?''

"I heard he stayed there, but even his girlfriend left with those other men, according to my informants.''

"Send some men who are calm to arrest him up there in the morning, and have him here to sit on the stand after the noon break tomorrow. He won't know what's been said before he got here, and you might trick him into admitting something.''

"Yes!'' Christianson said. "You better get some rest. You look pale.''

"I'll be all right,'' Slocum said, and rose from his seat. He dreaded the walk to Hap's small tent. But if he took his time he knew he could make it. A shame he didn't have a place of his own, but she had no aversion to him staying there, despite what it might do to her reputation.

Several men spoke to him as he walked steadily toward her tent. He managed to reach it, and stopped to rest on a bench inside.

"There you are, Your Honor,'' she said, spotting him. "You all right?''

"I'll be fine. First day—didn't get much done. We're going after it again tomorrow.''

"Are you going to make it through?''

"I have to. Maybe I'll go up to the small tent and rest a while.''

"Good idea,'' she said. "Need any help?''

"No,'' he said, and feeling somewhat rested from his sit-down, headed for the back of the tent. He had to get his strength back. He was weaker than a pup. The least exertion and he was done in. He could not survive at this rate if he was pressed.

Maybe it would get better. In the small tent he found his

things, and took a couple of jolts of rye from the neck of a bottle that he dug out of his saddlebags. Then he lay down on the new cot she had prepared for him. In minutes he was asleep in his clothing.

He woke at the sound of someone coughing. His hand closed on his Colt butt. He could make out the shadow of a man armed with a rifle. His silhouette was on the tent wall. Slocum rolled on his belly, and then off the cot onto his knees. Who was it? He swallowed hard. How many of them were there?

He cocked the hammer back and tried to listen. He could hear Hap's soft footfalls approaching. He needed to warn her—no, they might shoot her. What could he do?

"I've brought you something to eat. What's wrong?"

He held the gun barrel to his mouth to silence her. "Someone is out there." He jabbed the barrel in the direction of the armed man.

"Yes, I know," she said, holding out the plate of steaming meat and potatoes. "They are guarding you. Christianson sent them."

Slocum dropped his face on the cot. "Why didn't he say so?"

"You were sound asleep when they came. I thought it was a good idea."

"Yes, ma'am," he said, and rose up. He laid the Colt on the bed. "I woke up, saw his shadow on the tent, and figured it was someone after me."

"It's not. Here, eat this so you get well."

Seated on the bed, he took the meal in his lap. Guards were a good idea. If he couldn't defend himself, then he'd better have some guards.

"Do you need to get back to work?" he asked.

"No, I hired some help. Two of the miners' wives showed up and they're working for me. Supper is almost over. You've slept for a couple of hours up here."

"Doesn't feel like it. You met Buster Markley yet?"

"He ate a few times in the tent. Kind of a cocky fella, isn't he?"

"Yes, a good man to run a business, but not a socializer."

"He speak to you?"

"No, but you ought to have seen his face when he entered the courtroom and saw me."

"Shocked?"

"Very much so."

"How much does he owe you?"

"Around five hundred dollars." Slocum busied himself eating, having a better appetite than he expected.

"Can he pay you?"

"I doubt it. Probably gambled it away."

"Oh," she said, and took a seat next to him. She busied herself pushing his hair back from his face as he chewed on his meat. "It ain't worth fighting over."

"Oh, we'll see," he said between bites.

"I don't want to lose you, Slocum." She squeezed his good arm and laid her head on his shoulder.

"You don't know me. I'm a man on the run, Hap. If I implied or told you anything, then I'm sorry, but one day— any day—I'll have to leave and you won't be able to go with me."

"You can wire me. I'd come across a continent to be with you."

"Hap, you don't understand. There are men that want me. They'd watch your every move if they even thought you were going to meet me. They'd stop at nothing."

"I don't understand. . . ."

He looked at the canvas side of the tent bathed in the bloody red of the sundown. There were times when he didn't understand it all himself.

"When will these men come?" she asked in a soft voice.

He shook his head. "I don't ever know."

"I see," she said.

But he knew that she didn't. She hadn't seen the faded

posters of him that the two Abbot brothers carried in their saddlebags, heard the lies that had been testified to in that Fort Scott, Kansas, courtroom. A rich man's wild son had died, killed by a gun. A rich vindictive man who had the resources to keep up the chase even years later. And he paid the wages and expenses of the two men who rode the bounty trail for him.

Slocum knew them on sight. As sure as the sun came up in the morning, one day they would come riding into Owl Creek, looking for him. They had captured him on a half-dozen occasions, but he had always managed to escape, or had had assistance from a friend to get away.

Lyle and Dirk Abbot were out there somewhere like two bloodhounds on the track. All they needed was the scent of him.

16

"We've got to stop," the Kid called out.

"We can stop when we get there," Flannery said, glancing back at Lucy, who rode between them. "You making it?" he asked her.

"I could stand a short rest, but . . ." She looked at him, hoping that they could stop.

"Okay," Flannery said with an edge of disgust in his voice. "When we get on the next flat, we'll let the horses blow and take a break."

From their vantage point on the side of the mountain, he could see for miles to the distant ranges in the west. He hoped this narrow game trail would take them over the main spine of the Bradshaws and let them descend somewhere to the Black Canyon road. Down there they could find a stage stop and go on to the hay camp on the Salt River that they called Phoenix.

The narrow trail at last hit a flat, and he reined in his horse. He dismounted heavily and went to help her off her horse.

"Where are we?" she asked privately.

"Somewhere in the Bradshaw Mountains, headed for a

stage line that will take us miles from those miners.''

''I need to . . .'' She looked around with a frown.

''Go anywhere. We won't look,'' he said.

''I don't care who watches. I simply need to do it.''

Lucy rushed off as the Kid waded over to the side to relieve himself behind a pine tree. His paint horse, with his head hung low, snorted in the dust. They needed a place to rest up. Flannery didn't know the mountains, only the general direction of things that men had mentioned to him.

''We still eating crackers and cheese?'' the Kid asked, coming across the flat to where he stood.

''That's all we've got. Unless you got some highfalutin stuff with you,'' Flannery said.

''I ain't got a damn thing. Can we stay here?''

''No. We need to get on and find some water.''

''Where's that?''

''Somewhere over this range, I guess.''

''I don't know, I'm worn out,'' the Kid complained.

''You'd get some lead out of your ass if you knew them miners was coming after you.''

''I don't think they're coming after us.'' The Kid sneered in disbelief.

''We'll see. I ain't going to be here for them to take me back. She's coming,'' he said.

''We going on?'' she asked.

''Yes,'' he said, and helped her into the saddle. The smell of her perfume made a knot in his stomach as he considered her body under his hands. He had lots to live for yet; Lucy's body was damn sure one of them.

By late afternoon, they struck a trail with dim horse prints. The find made Flannery feel easier. Someone on horseback or leading horses had been over this way, and that meant there was a way out, not some goat path like the one they'd followed so far.

In a short time, they passed over the top, Flannery decided, and at last they were looking out at new saw-edged mountains in the east. Good, they must be on the Black Canyon side of the range.

Further down the trail, he rounded a bend in the track, and the sun on a glass pane blinded him for a second. There under the trees sat a small neat log cabin. He could hardly believe his eyes.

"My gosh, who lives up here?" Lucy asked.

"I'm not certain." He reached for his gun, then reined his horse in to take a closer look at the place.

"Anyone there?" the Kid asked, squinting in the red light of sundown.

"Nothing in the corral," Flannery said. "Ride up slow. Maybe they're about the place."

They rode three abreast to the door. No sign of a soul. The Kid dismounted, went to the door, and knocked. No one came, so he pulled the door string and the door swung open. He stuck his head inside. Then he came out.

"Neat as a pin, but ain't a soul here." He shook his head in disbelief.

"There's a well out back. If there's any water in it, we better draw some up for these animals," Flannery said.

"Would it be all right to go inside?" she asked meekly.

"I don't know why not," Flannery said, and dismounted to help her down.

"Who do you figure owns the place?" the Kid asked, looking around. "They did lots of work and that cabin is nice inside."

"No telling. It looks like heaven to me," Flannery said, and dropped the bucket down the well, holding the tail of the rope. The splash made them both smile.

"Here, I'll draw it up," the Kid said, and took the rope from him.

Flannery began to breathe easier. The heavy feeling in his chest flew away. If he'd ever prayed, his prayers had been answered. They had a comfortable hideout for a few days, and at last he had Lucy for himself.

"Kid, mind if Lucy and me stay in the cabin?" He

looked at him hard, so he would get his drift.

"Yeah, I know. You want her for yourself, don't you?" He dumped the water pail in the log trough, and the thirsty horses drew it up in a few slurps.

"Maybe later."

"All right, but I want some too. I'll sleep out here." He looked up. "Here she comes."

"Mick," she said, excited. "I found three cans of tomatoes. If we left the money for them, could we drink them?"

"Sure, we can do that," he said, excited at the notion of having a can of tomatoes to himself. Only a few hours ago all he could think about was the dry crackers he carried in his saddlebags. He drew out his jackknife and shared a nod of approval with Kid. No need to leave money for someone not there, but he sure would do about anything to please her.

He punched holes in her can first. She grinned as she lifted it up, and the red juice leaked around the corner of her mouth until she took the can down and gasped for her breath.

"Gawdamn, boys, that is better than French champagne." With a rusty mustache of juice on her upper lip, she grinned at them, and they returned the smile. Then she went back for more, slurping it noisily.

"Well, ain't you going to drink yours?" she asked with a questioning frown.

"Yeah. We kinda enjoying watching you drink yours," Flannery said, and then he punched holes in the other two cans.

The first salty mouthful of the cool contents did taste better to him than any sugar drink he'd ever had, including icy lemonade. It must have been cool in the cabin where the cans had been stored. Man, it was good for his dry throat. He put his can down, and cut open the lid on hers so she could fish out the whole tomatoes.

With the first ball of red held between her fingers, she

winked at him wickedly, then began to consume it. He felt himself getting hard. How long had he wanted her? Since Burns had first showed up with her on his arm in Yuma. He could hardly wait for the night. Unable to take his eyes off her, he finished the juice in his can and then he cut open the top.

In the fleeting orange sunlight, he stabbed himself a tomato and then popped it in whole. The acid salty taste flooded his entire mouth with a richness that few things besides peaches could ever match. Slowly his teeth chewed it as he studied her hips and considered how she looked under the skirt.

"I guess I better finish watering these horses," the Kid said, sounding disgusted over having to work, and dropped the pail back in the well.

"I guess this is our supper?" she asked Flannery.

"Filled me up."

"Me too," she said.

"You did great finding them," he said, uncinching the horse.

"Oh, I thought it would be a nice treat for all of us."

"It was, Lucy," the Kid said as he pulled up more water hand over hand. "Wonder how he got a well up here in the first place."

"It's a cistern, catches rainwater," Flannery said, unsaddling her horse and putting the rig on the corral. "There ain't no wells this high up."

"Then there ain't going to be no big supply down in it?"

"No. When you use it up, you've got to wait for another rain."

The Kid leaned over the log casing and tried to see down into it.

"You still getting bucketsful?" Flannery asked.

"Yeah, but—"

"Don't worry about it. Just water the horses. Here, Lucy,

I can get that bucket for you,'' he said as she brought an empty one from the house.

''I figured we needed one to make coffee with.''

''Coffee in there?'' he asked, holding the bucket as the Kid poured it full.

''There's tea. I found some in a tin.''

Flannery carried the pail, and she walked with him back to the cabin, talking about the cabin's contents.

Inside, he had to agree that it was the neatest place he'd ever been in. It was so isolated and obscure that he might have ridden by if the light had not reflected off the small pane. He glanced at the bed. A mattress over a rope frame.

''See the irons in the fireplace?'' She pointed them out to him. ''Who owns this place?''

''Lucy, I don't care who owns it,'' he said, putting the water pail on the table. ''For now it is ours to use.''

She blinked her eyelashes and then frowned at him. ''What do you mean?''

''I mean I been wanting you ever since I first laid eyes on you in Yuma that day.''

''You have?'' She smiled, pleased.

''Why, Lucy,'' he said, and pulled her into his embrace, ''I've been wanting you forever.''

''Gosh, Flannery, that's the nicest thing anyone ever said to me.''

''Aw, it ain't,'' he said as she played with the front of his shirt.

''It sure is. What are we waiting for?'' she asked.

''Damned if I know.''

''Let's take our clothes off then.''

''Sure,'' he said, not ready to believe her words.

Clothes flew everywhere. She tore off her blouse and threw it aside. He did the same with his coat and vest. And they stomped around the room after each other like Indians at a war dance. She had the riding skirt off in the shake of a lamb's tail, and he had his pants undone. But he had to stop, sit on the floor, and unbutton his shoes to get the britches off. The delay pissed him off.

By then she was dancing around in her corset. Her short legs flashed as she kicked his coat and vest up in the air. He could hardly believe any woman was that spirited.

"Can you undo my corset?" she asked, backing up to him. His hands clasped her thighs, and he felt like doing a fling himself with her silky flesh in his grasp.

"Sure," he said, and his trembling hands began to unlace the corset. How long could he control himself?

When she undid the corset, his hands cupped her small soft breasts from behind. He pressed himself against her butt and rested his face on top of her head. The light in the cabin grew dimmer as he aroused her nipples with his fingertips.

"You ready?" she asked.

"Yes."

"Come on, get that underwear off then," she said, and he hurried to obey.

She crossed the room and lay down on the bed. He stripped off the top portion of his underwear and took the legs off inside out, hobbling around the floor. Damn things anyway. At last, stark naked, he hurried to the side of the bed.

The sharp pain in his chest made him wince as he put his knee on the bed. He could see the black mound of hair below her belly—no damn hairless sewed-up Chinese crotch. His heart began to thump harder as he moved between her short legs and reached down to pull on his aching cock.

"Oh," he said. "I've waited a long time for this."

"So have I," she whispered. Her hands were on the outside of his arms, gliding over them—making goose flesh on his skin.

Shaking with his need for her, he nosed his root in her wet door, and then realized what was happening. He cried out in protest as his body double-crossed him. His hips tried to launch him deeper inside her as the head of his shaft exploded. His eyes squeezed shut, and he held himself suspended over her as his stalk wilted.

"That's all right, honey," she said, consoling him. "We'll get him ready again. You lay down here with me."

He dropped to the bed beside her, but he knew the task was impossible. Her small fingers manipulated him. They pulled on it, and with her nails she scratched the crown of it. Still, despite the small pleasure of her touch, nothing stirred him to another erection.

"You're just tired," she said. "Sleep for a while and we can do it when you're rested."

Flannery agreed. He could sleep. His heart only ached by this time. She was right. A little rest and he could do it and do it to her until she cried that she'd had enough. He had done other women in the past like that—he was out of practice, that was all. He closed his eyes, and sleep quickly took him away.

Sometime in the night, he awoke. She was not in the bed when he felt for her. He wondered where she had gone. The pressure on his bladder was so bad he had to get up, go outside, and piss. The cool air washed over his skin as he went to the open door.

He stood on the porch in his bare feet and listened. He could hear someone giggling, and he froze. A frown formed as he considered what would be so damn funny at this time of the night. The Kid—she and the gawdamn Kid were playing games in the middle of the night? He eased himself to the edge of the cabin to look around the corner, and squinted to see in the pearly starlight.

He could hardly believe his eyes. There they were in the clearing on the ground on hands and knees and naked— like two dogs. The Kid's skinny butt was pumping her from behind. Flannery blinked in disbelief.

She kept snickering as if the Kid was tickling her. That

horny son of a bitch—he ought to go pistol-whip him. He'd
told him that she was his.

"Do it faster," she said out loud.

"I'm trying," the Kid complained, out of breath.

He always complained. Flannery shook his head, and
then he went quietly to the other side of the cabin to relieve
himself. Finished, he went back to bed and stared at the
ceiling and listened, catching small phrases of what they
said and more of her giggles. He rolled over and tried to
shut it out. Later, he fell asleep.

17

The plans were made after breakfast. Christianson and the six other members of the miners committee all met with Slocum in the saloon.

"So you don't want Burns brought in until after lunch?" the big man behind the walrus mustache asked. Clarence Wallen had been chosen to be the head deputy in the arrest of Burns.

"Right, Clarence," Christianson answered. "Timing is important. He won't know what's been said, so we might trick him into admitting his part in all this business."

"I doubt it. He ain't no fool," Slocum said. No need for them to think this Burns would be a simpleton. "I figure that he's been paying them three to do his dirty work the whole time."

"Did any of you ever see that little gal who lived with him?" a younger man asked. "Whew, she was a looker." He dropped his chin and then shook his head in disbelief.

"She ran off with Flannery, they say," Wallen replied

"She did?" the young man asked. "I wanted to arrest her." He grinned, and the others laughed.

"No word back from the posse yet?" Clarence asked.

Slocum shook his head. "Those three had a big head start."

"They won't lose that hunter Duggan."

"No, they won't do that. We were lucky he went along with the posse," Slocum agreed. His shoulder hurt less than any morning since the shooting. He sipped the coffee in his cup as Christianson went over his plan to have the Chinese girl testify.

"Didn't Lou Wee work for Burns at one time?" Slocum asked. "The Kid came and tried to get her back. Have you asked her anything about Flannery and Burns?"

"No," Christianson said. "But I will on the stand."

"Court in an hour," Slocum announced.

"You ever do any law business before this?" Clarence asked him.

Slocum shook his head.

"You sure do it good."

The others agreed, and prepared to leave.

Alone at last, Slocum considered the session ahead. He had tried on the night of his return to get them to make someone else the judge, but they wouldn't listen. What would they do if they knew the whole truth about his past? Probably nothing—he had no accusers in this camp.

Court went according to plan. A jury of twelve miners was seated on chairs to one side of the room. Christianson explained that they were to listen to the evidence and decide who the guilty parties were.

Two men testified to how they had removed Swenson's dead body from Flannery's shack.

"How did he look?" Christianson asked the second man. "When you carried him out."

"He looked blue. I mean, blue in the face like he had no air. You know what I mean?"

"Yes, we do. You are excused."

Lou Wee took the stand. Her voice was so low that no one dared scuff their feet on the floor for fear of missing a word that she said.

"I come on big ship to America," she said. Her answers were short and to the point.

"I go to work one day. That man, Flannery, he grab me. He hold hand over mouth, drag me in bushes, tie my hands, use rag on my mouth, carry me to his place."

"Miss Wee, did anyone in any way hurt you?"

She looked at Slocum and made a face as if undecided whether to continue or not. He nodded for her to go on.

"The Kid?" she said.

"Yes," Christianson said, almost breathless.

"He stick his big thing up my ass." She rose and pointed demonstratively toward her butt. "He do it many times. Hurt me." Then she sat down.

The roar of protest by the audience forced Slocum to pound his gavel for order. It required several minutes for the wave of noisy anger and threats toward the Kid to subside. At last, with order restored, Slocum nodded for the prosecutor to continue.

"Did Flannery do anything to you like that?" Christianson asked.

"He tried." She wrinkled her small nose.

"He tried what, Miss Wee?"

"He tried to stick it in me in front." She leaned back and pointed to her lap, then made a distasteful face and continued. "But he was too soft and then he come all over belly." She held her hands up as if there was nothing she could do about the mess.

Her words brought laughter to the crowd. Slocum pounded the gavel for order.

Next, Christianson had her talk about Flannery and the Kid bringing in the dazed Swenson. And after several more questions, he posed the big one to her. What had she seen?

"Me see that man Flannery, he hold pillow on big man's face until he not kick no more."

"The Kid helped him?"

"Yes."

The murmur of the miners was loud.

"Your Honor," Christianson said, turning to Slocum. "May I suggest we recess for lunch."

"Recess until one o'clock," Slocum pounded the gavel.

"They've got Burns!" someone shouted, and the miners rushed outside to see the prisoner.

"Well, you make a very impressive judge," Markley said, standing next to the bench.

"Thanks. You have anything to say for yourself?" Slocum asked, standing up.

"About our deal?" Markley held on to the lapels of his frock coat.

"Yes."

"Had a run of bad luck." He shrugged as if that would answer it. "We lost too much money on the gambling operation one night."

"Damn strange. Sure you didn't personally lose too much?"

"You accusing me?"

"You left no word. As I recall, I had a stake in that place."

"I suppose you want your investment back."

"It would be fair enough." Slocum looked up as the court deputies dragged in the red-faced Burns bound hand and foot in ropes.

"He didn't want to come," Clarence said, and had his men seat Burns in a front-row chair.

"This is no court of law!" Burns shouted.

Slocum shook his head and ignored the man's vocal protests. He turned back to Markley. "You were saying?"

"I figured easy come, easy go."

"Five hundred dollars," Slocum said slowly. Markley wasn't getting off the hook that easily. He'd never bothered to come tell Slocum, nor had he even sent word.

"I don't have that much money," Markley said. "I don't even know where I can get that much." He shifted his boots.

"Borrow it from your bosses."

"You invested, you lost."

"Markley, I invested in a business, not your poker playing."

"All right, I'll find some money to pay you."

"When?"

"I came to apologize." His dark eyes were slits of burning anger.

"I'll take my money instead, thanks," Slocum said, and left the man standing there. He could feel the daggers in his back as he headed out the door. His appetite was much improved. The arm was still in a sling, but it hurt less this day than any other. Maybe he was healing at last. From the corner of his eye, he saw Markley hurrying off. The man would bear close watching.

18

"How long we staying here?" the Kid asked, looking hungover as he came inside the cabin. His black eye was about half open and the bruises from the beating had faded, but he still looked half asleep.

"I ain't sure," Flannery said from his seat across from Lucy at the table. There was no way he could ride far this day. He was so light-headed, he felt uncertain that he could even stay in the saddle. His heart was acting up too, had been since he awoke. But he wouldn't dare tell them a thing about that. The sharp pains in his arm and chest were distracting. Maybe he should go see a doctor in Phoenix. These days they had medicine for things that went wrong with your body.

"You don't think them miners will chase us this far?" the Kid asked.

"Yeah, I do. Why don't you go back down the trail and look off the top into that canyon we come up yesterday. See if they are coming."

"All right," the Kid said, and frowned at having to do the task.

"I'll saddle the horses and be ready to move in case they are coming," Flannery said.

"Won't take me long."

"Look real good for them," Flannery said after him. "Take your rifle."

"I will." The Kid left them, scuffing his boot heels as he disappeared with the Winchester out the front door.

"What are you going to do?" Lucy asked him. "I mean, when we get away from here?"

"Buy me a saloon of my own. I've got the money to do it." He had that in his pants pockets, thanks to Swenson and the saloon bank of Burns.

"Need a partner?" she asked, busy filing her pink fingernails.

"I guess. You interested?"

"Sure. What will we call it?" she asked, blowing on the nails.

"The Shamrock. That's Irish lucky clover."

"I know what a shamrock is. Sounds okay."

"You got a better name for it?"

"No. Where we going in business at?"

"I was thinking maybe in Globe—they got a big copper strike up there."

"Yeah, these gold and silver camps are all kind of primitive." She made a sour face.

The sounds of shots made him jump up. The miners must be coming. He had horses to saddle. The quickness of his movements made his head swirl. He caught himself on the door jamb and tried to blink the dizziness away.

"They're coming, aren't they?" she asked in a hushed voice beside him.

"Yeah, or he stopped them. Got to . . . saddle the horses."

"Are you all right, Mick?"

"I will be. Just this high altitude makes me dizzy is all."

She caught the horses and led them over to him. He managed to pad and saddle them, still looking and listening for the Kid to return. He should have been back by this time—unless they'd shot him.

He boosted her in the saddle. "Ride. I'll check on the Kid and then catch up."

"Think something happened to him?" she asked with a worried frown.

"I'm not sure."

"Be careful. I could never get out of here by myself."

"Follow the trail. If I don't come, you'll find someone."

She looked toward the south with concern. "I hope he's all right."

"Yeah, we may need him later," Flannery said, holding his breath against the pain in his upper body and mounting up. He caught the reins to the paint and then, leading it, booted his horse to make him go. What had happened to that damn Kid anyway?

Flannery rode down the trail, listening and wondering if he was riding into a trap. Then he saw the Kid coming in a hurry with the Winchester. He looked okay.

"What happened?" Flannery asked, handing him the reins to his paint.

"They were halfway up the mountain. I got two of them and three of their horses." The Kid was wide-eyed and obviously shaken by his encounter.

"You recognize who they were?" he asked as the Kid mounted up.

"One was that hunter Duggan."

"You get him?"

"Yeah, I'm pretty sure he's one I got. Let's get the hell out of here."

"Good, he'd be the worst one of all of them to track us down." Flannery could not see back down in the canyon for the trees and the rock face between him and the other side of the mountain. No time for that anyway. They needed to vamoose. But if the Kid got Duggan, they could still manage to get away. He sure hoped the Kid wasn't just talking through his hat and had really hit the man.

They hurried their mounts, and caught up with Lucy. She looked wide-eyed at them.

"What happened?" she asked.

"They were closer than we thought, but the Kid stopped them."

"Oh, my God," she said, and turned pale. "I wonder if they've got Burns."

"Hell, he stayed there," Flannery said, and whipped his horse to trot faster. "It's his own dumb fault if he got caught."

"Did this man Flannery work for you?" Christianson asked Burns as he sat with his arms folded over his chest in the witness chair.

"No!" Burns snapped.

"Why did Miss Wee say that he did?"

"I don't care what that slant-eyed bitch told you. Flannery never worked for me." He looked smug and angry, staring off over the crowd at something on the back wall of the saloon.

"I have here," Christianson said, "a deed to Swenson's claim made out to you. Can you explain that?"

"Who's Swenson?" Burns grumbled.

"Mr. Swenson was the man that was murdered."

"I didn't do it."

"Did your man Flannery do it?"

"How should I know? He don't work for me. Ask him."

"We will when the posse brings him in. Is he going to tell us that you ordered the murder?"

"I don't know Flannery."

"Miss Wee says he came and asked you what to do when she worked for your lady."

"Chinese lie all the damn time. Their testimony ain't even admissable in a real court of law."

"I don't think that she lied. Mr Burns, did you kill Charlie McRoy?"

"No."

"How come you are working and living on his claim?"

"Free country." Burns shrugged it away like a gnat.

"We call it claim-jumping."

"You got proof I did that?"

"Charlie McRoy had a claim on that property. He's murdered and you moved in."

"I didn't kill him."

"You did jump his claim."

"People do that all the time. One man moves on, someone else moves in and digs. That's not a crime."

"It is in Owl Creek."

"Who cares." He shook his head to dismiss both Christianson and Slocum.

"Gentlemen of the court," Christianson said to the jury. "You've heard the man's answers to the charge of the murder of Olaf Swenson. You've heard his answers to the demise of Charlie McRoy and his opinion concerning claim rights. With that I rest my case." Christenson turned to Slocum. "Your Honor, the prosecution rests."

"Mr. Burns, what do you have to say before the jury deliberates your fate?" Slocum said.

"You ain't got any authority to try me, and I never killed no one."

"Mr. Burns, is that all you have to say? I must tell you that these are serious charges and the consequences could be even more so." Slocum hoped to impress the man that his life was at stake.

"You want me to beg?" Burns refolded his arms and curled his lip in disgust.

"No, sir. I shall excuse the jury to deliberate the matter of guilt or innocence."

The jury rose and went outside. Slocum wondered how long they would be gone. He could see the indignation of Burns as he straightened up his suit and tie and squirmed uncomfortably in the seat.

"How did you get in charge of this kangaroo court?" Burns asked Slocum.

"He was elected," Christianson said.

"Yeah, elected." Then suddenly Burns whirled around

as the jury filed back in and took their seats.

"How do you find the defendant Harvey Burns?" Slocum asked.

"Guilty as sin," the jury foreman said. "We think he should be hung with Flannery and the Kid."

"What?!" Burns screamed. He began to shout and stomp his foot with his tirade.

Slocum pounded the gavel for order, and finally rose and aimed it toward Burns. "You shut up or I shall have you gagged.

"By the order of this miners court, I order you, Harvey Burns, to be sentenced to hang for the murders of Charlie McRoy and Olaf Swenson and for claim-jumping. That execution shall take place in the morning."

"You can't do this to me!"

"Guards, take him to the shack and keep him there until sunrise," Slocum ordered. "At that time we should have a scaffold erected."

"We will have it ready," several men said as Slocum banged the gavel for adjournment.

Slocum felt pleased that the case was over. He rose stiffly to his feet.

"That means we also tried Flannery and the Kid for those crimes?" Christianson asked under his breath as they headed for Hap's.

"I would say so, unless you want to ask a jury about the rape of the girl."

Christenson shook his head. "Hanging is good enough for me. How is the shoulder?"

"Better," Slocum lied. At that moment it hurt him worse than it had all day.

"What are you going to do when this is over?"

"Finish building Hap's kitchen, I guess, if I ever get so I can use my bad arm."

"You should run for judge. You'd make a good one. Never lost your temper, never raised your voice. I was impressed with your control."

"Thanks, but I better stick to things I know," Slocum said as they reached Hap's big tent.

"I heard the verdict," she said, looking at him. "They must have run down here to tell me. Do you think he did it?"

Slocum nodded. "Those men worked for him. He must have known about it."

"I guess we'll really have the hangings if they get those other two back here."

"I expect Duggan will get them."

"Hungry?" she asked.

Slocum shook his head. He wanted a drink of good whiskey and time to think about the entire day. Life or death—a decision he neither liked nor relished having a hand in. In a court of law, Burns would have had hired high-priced legal experts and they'd have talked circles around Christianson. More than likely, he'd have gotten off.

What had Duggan said? They needed a miners court to decide the issue of guilt or innocence?

"I'm going inside," Slocum said, and then turned to Christianson. "You want a good drink?"

"Yes, I do."

In the privacy of the tent, Slocum undid his shirt and with care took his arm from the sling. Christianson poured the whiskey in the glasses on the table. Slocum's limb was still stiff in the socket and elbow. It hurt from lack of use, but he began to flex it despite the pain.

"Can you use it?" Christianson asked, looking up.

"Some."

"Slocum, come quick," Hap said from the end of the tent. "The posse's back and they've been shot up."

Both men exchanged questioning looks, and then rose to go see. Duggan was riding double, and had his head wrapped in a kerchief under his hat.

"What happened?" Slocum asked.

"They doubled back, I guess," Duggan said. "We had almost caught up with them about sunup when one of them opened fire on us. They got Little Ira, creased Loftin in the ribs, and killed three good horses.''

"They crease you?" Slocum asked as the man dismounted.

"Came close," Duggan said, and helped the wounded man off his horse.

"You didn't get a shot at them?"

Duggan shook his head. "We were in the open on a mountainside. But I think we can take a shortcut to Crown King and cut them off."

"You able to ride?" Slocum asked.

"Hell, that's just a scratch," the hunter said, indicating his bandaged head. "I'm fine. We need to go back after them."

"Yes. I'm glad they didn't shoot my dun," Slocum said, looking him over. "He'll make the ride."

"We'll get Duggan a fresh horse," someone said.

"Slocum!" Hap called. With her dress in her hands, she rushed to catch up with him.

"You can't go," she said, surprised that he would even consider such a task. "Why you're—one-handed. Let someone else go."

"No. These miners are men who work with their muscles and backs, not guns. Besides, I have a stake in this. I'm convinced that I owe Flannery for this shoulder."

"Why can't I ever talk you out of doing crazy things?" she asked in defeat.

"Same reason that you don't listen to me."

"Hardheadedness?"

"Yes. We both have it." One-handed, he started to lengthen the stirrups. She stepped in and took over the job. He shared a warm smile with her as he tightened the cinch. Tough woman, Hap Arnold. If he only had more time for her. Maybe later—one day, when things leveled out in his life.

19

"Are they coming?" Lucy asked. Her once-fine curls were hanging limp in her face as she sat on the log. Her dress was hiked up to expose her white legs, and she looked the picture of total dejection.

"No sign of anyone," the Kid said, dismounting. "How's Mick?"

"He's inside sick. I covered him up. Something's bad wrong with him. He says his chest hurts him."

"Well, that's a fine mess. He takes sick and them miners are hot after us."

"He ain't fooling," she said.

"Maybe some whiskey would help him."

"You got any?"

"He usually does in his saddlebags."

"I'll go look."

Inside the cabin, Mick wanted to say the pain would pass. It always did. Only this time it had been so bad he'd fainted. He'd been sending the Kid out to check on their backtrail when the lights had gone out. He'd awakened to hear them talking about him.

154

"I'll be fine," he said as they came in the cabin, and they both started as he threw off the blanket, sat up, and began rubbing his face in his palms. "It's the damn altitude up here."

"Yeah, well, you scared the shit out of me," Lucy said, and began to fold the blanket.

"I didn't do it on purpose," Mick said to soothe her. "What did you learn?" he asked the Kid.

"I went back to where I could see lots of that mountain we came from. They ain't in sight, and there ain't no smoke if they made camp."

"Good. We can't be far from Crown King."

"More sign of travel on this trail," the Kid agreed. He stopped and turned his head. Someone was singing. He drew his gun, but Flannery managed to push the muzzle down.

"Probably some old prospector coming up the trail. He ain't no harm," he said. "Besides, he may know the shortest way to Crown King."

"Yeah," the Kid agreed, and holstered his gun.

Lucy busied herself brushing her hair. Then she straightened her blouse and the waist of her skirt. Flannery went outside and tied the blanket on her horse. The Kid and Lucy followed him out. Flannery kept glancing in the direction of the singing and the sound of approaching burro hooves.

"Well, howdy, folks," the man of medium build said from behind a bushy white beard and mustache. He removed his peaked felt hat and made a bow for Lucy.

"Handsome lady, me name is Gurdy. And the likes of you I seldom see on this pathway through the sky."

"Lucy's mine," she said, acting almost uncomfortable at the attention he showered on her.

"And you lads be going back or coming this way?" The man looked at the two of them with interest.

"We need to get to Crown King," Flannery said.

"Ah, Crown King. Yes, a fine spot of civilization in this rugged pinery, I'd say."

"How many miles away is it?" Flannery asked.

" 'Tis not far. Depends, though. On those steeds of yours, you could be there by the morrow."

"A day's ride then?" Flannery asked.

"On this trail."

"Is there another trail we should take?" Flannery asked, growing angry with the man's blathering.

"Not unless you got wings."

"Keep going north, huh?"

"Ah, yes, go north. But the lady—Crown King has few amenities for such a lady."

"She'll be fine," Flannery said, much of his pain gone. He mounted up. "Thanks, Gurdy."

"Thank you very much," Lucy said, and kissed him on the forehead.

"Aye, I have been touched by the heavens. Here, take this pouch of dust and buy yourself new finery, my lady." He drew it from his ragged canvas coat pocket.

Flannery looked on in disbelief. Then he booted his horse in close as she opened the drawstrings on the buckskin pouch. The glitter of gold caught his breath. Lucy drew it shut, shoved it with some effort between her breasts, then grabbed the man by his arms and kissed him all over his face.

"She gets done kissing that old goat, you help her up on her horse," Flannery said to the Kid.

"Whoopee!" the man cried out, and did a jig in the open space. Flannery last saw Gurdy whirling his hat over his head and having himself a fit jumping around in the gray sagebrush. Then Flannery pushed his horse up the trail into the pines again.

How much gold was in that pouch? No matter how much there was in that pouch, they both were partners. They'd need it later for their saloon, and he'd get it from her then. The old fool—plain stupid giving gold away like that to some whore who'd kissed him. Men had no sense at all. Flannery rubbed his breastbone. He was sore as ever inside.

• • •

They rode all day, and at dusk rode into a mining operation. Several dusty rock miners greeted them coldly. Flannery doubted he and the Kid could have found any welcome, but when the miners spotted Lucy, things warmed up.

"Where you headed?" a white-toothed miner asked her, coming at a run to walk beside her. Ladies' man—Flannery could tell the type.

"Crown King," she said as demurely as a pure virgin.

"Why don't you stop and spend the night here?" the man asked.

"My—ah, friends. Flannery, can we stop?"

"Sure," he said, and looked at the man.

"Get down. We shot a deer yesterday so we have lots of food," the man said. "You're welcome to join in."

The man took her down from the horse with his hands on her waist. Easily he swung her out of the saddle and set her on the ground; his eyes glistened as he looked into hers. A twinge of jealousy struck Flannery like a sledgehammer. This dandy wasn't getting her all night like the Kid had the night before.

Flannery moved in, took Lucy's arm, and told the Kid to put up their horses. The man nodded that he understood when Flannery took possession of her. She was his and that was that.

The other miners were grateful for a look at such a beautiful woman. They removed their hats and gathered around to shake her hand like hound-dog pups waiting for scraps at a back door.

"Name's Tobin," a young man said, and he showed them to crude log benches. Then someone began to bring the food from the fire ring. The men hung back, and Tobin told her to fill a metal plate first.

Graciously she rose and with Flannery on her heels, she went through the serving line, which was set up on the split-log table. She selected some meat on bones from the first pot, then dipped out steaming red beans from the next pot. Flannery did the same, and armed with a spoon apiece, they sat down. The food smelled good enough. He hoped it didn't give him diarrhea, but he was hungry enough to eat anything.

"Where do you live?" Tobin asked, seated across from her. He had taken a bone with meat from his plate and was ready to chew the meat off.

"Oh, we move around a lot," she said.

"Where would you like to live?" he asked, not bothering to start on his meal.

"San Fransisco, I guess."

"I'm going there next year," he said.

"Oh? To live?" she asked.

"I think so. This mine is just a way station in my life."

"A way station?" she asked.

"He's saying that he has other means of support," Flannery stuck in between bites of his food. Not bad-tasting at all.

"What do you mean?" she asked, pained.

"He's rich."

"Well, not quite," Tobin said, acting uncomfortable at the notion.

"My, do you have a family somewhere?" she asked.

"In Virginia. Sterling, Virginia."

"I see," she said as she set her spoon down and then wiped the corners of her mouth with her kerchief.

None of this was missed by Flannery. She was really good. She had Tobin eating out of her hand. Yes, she would do as a partner. What would this Tobin pay to sleep with her? Maybe a lot of money or gold if his claim was producing. They could use lots of money to start their new business. Not such a poor idea either. Tobin couldn't wear her out if the Kid hadn't the night before. That gawdamn Kid had tried hard enough to do that.

20

Slocum could see for miles from the side of the mountain. This shortcut that Duggan had chosen looked like little more than a bighorn-sheep trail. The dun horse was sure-footed, so Slocum put his trust in him as they wound their way upward. Still one-handed, he was forced to catch his balance from time to time and rein the dun with his left hand. Both riders moved single file around some tight places along the sheer wall where the alternate way was a thousand feet of space—straight down.

"It ain't far now," Duggan would often say over his shoulder, and every time all Slocum could see was the towering face the trail clung to. Even the buzzards flew below them. He had seen several of them gliding along under them.

What if? Slocum had considered it several times. What if this dim trail petered out. There was no way to back down it as far as they had already come without finding a landing or a spot wide enough for a man to dismount. His left boot was wedged between the horse and the bluffs's face, and his other boot hung out over eternity. But Duggan claimed to know the way, and Slocum trusted him. The hunter had never mentioned how many times he had used this way of getting to Crown King. All he had said was, "I know a shortcut and we can beat them there."

Slocum tried to keep his mind distracted. He studied the granite spires that rose in columns for hundreds of feet and sparkled as if loaded with riches. He knew it was only flecks of feldspar, but they resembled diamonds and the glitter of gold in the sunlight.

The two horses' iron shoes clicked on the rocks. The metallic ring tolled like a bell, and then re-echoed in the vast space of thin air. Despite the cool breeze on his face, Slocum's armpits were soaked, and he repeatedly dried his left palm on his pants. His hatband was lubricated by perspiration, and he leaned forward so as to not stop the dun with the reins. Then he reached up with the same hand that held the reins, doffed the hat, and used the opportunity to wipe his gritty face on his sleeve. He replaced the hat, but not before he noticed the ledge had grown narrower.

The dun hesitated, lowered his nose, and snorted wearily at the gap in the shelf. Then, without urging, he made a half jump to the next part of the shelf. Slocum's heart stopped. When the dun landed, his right hind hoof scrambled under him for footing. The horse's torso listed dangerously to the off side as he sought a place for his hoof. The shoe clacked as he repeatedly slid off the edge. Slocum leaned against the wall and held his breath. Seconds passed like hours. Then, with effort, the dun's shoe rang out. At last, he'd found a solid place. For a long moment, horse and rider stopped, unmoving, and drew in short breaths.

A shiver of cold ran up Slocum's spine. He felt the dun horse start to move under him again, and he exhaled in relief. When he looked up ahead, he saw a bushy juniper growing out of the rock and blocking the path ahead for Duggan. They had come all this way and at last were stymied. He shut his eyes to block out the consequences.

"We've made it," Duggan shouted back.

Yeah, they sure had. They could stay up there until they

starved or fell asleep and then rolled off the mountain. They had made it, all right. He shook his head in defeat. He'd made some damn poor choices in his life, but this one had to been the worst.

He looked up, and then he blinked. Duggan and his horse had disappeared from sight. Slocum glanced off the side. Had they fallen over without him seeing it? Where were they?

Another fifty feet up the steep path and he would be there. Maybe he could learn where they had vanished. He could feel the dun begin to tire. He kept snorting and blowing. Where in the hell had Duggan and his horse gone?

His pony gathered himself, and had to hump up to climb the last twenty feet. This section proved to be as steep as a cow's face. Slocum had to lean forward in the saddle to help the dun and to keep himself from falling out in the lurches.

Then the dun nickered softly and turned sharply into a side canyon. Ahead of them, dismounted and mopping his face with his kerchief, stood Duggan. The narrow chasm boasted a flat floor, and Slocum dropped gratefully to the ground. Then, for a long moment, braced against the horse, he closed his eyes and thanked his guardian angel—one more time.

One more time he had been saved from the jaws of death.

"Helluva trail, huh?" Duggan said.

"Tough one."

"Every time I have to use it, I swear I'm never coming this way again."

"What would have happened if it had ended?"

"I wondered about that myself." Duggan shook his head. "But I'll bet that we'll sure beat them to Crown King."

Slocum looked back to the yawning mouth of the canyon and the open azure sky beyond. He sure hoped so after all that.

The rest of the way proved easy. It was steep in places,

climbing up on the benches, but under the tall pine canopy, with the first branches twenty feet up, they rode eastward at a good trot without obstructions.

They reached Crown King at sundown. Both men dismounted in front of the Lady Luck Saloon and glanced around. A cluster of saloons and stores lined the crooked hilly main street under some remaining pines.

"I ain't seen that Kid's paint," Duggan offered.

"He's not hitched on the street," Slocum added after a final careful check.

"Let's get us a drink and some food. This place is the best one for food. And maybe someone in here's seen them."

Slocum agreed, and mounted the porch with some effort. He still was not satisfied. Besides the Kid's paint, he wanted to be sure there was not another familiar horse hitched in the street.

"You ready to go in?" Duggan asked.

"Sure," Slocum said, and took the bat-wing door in his left hand, twisting to keep his sore right shoulder from hitting the other side.

"Welcome to Crown King, gents," a short skinny bar girl said with a big smile. She was hardly out of her teens, her low-cut blouse exposing her small cleavage as she stood with her feet apart blocking their way.

"What will it be, gents?" she asked.

"A big steak for each of us and a bottle of . . ." Duggan turned to Slocum with a questioning look.

"Rye will be fine."

"I've got that coming," she said. "Have you a seat, gents. How about some female company?" she asked with a sly smile.

Duggan shook his head, and then looked at Slocum, who confirmed it. They didn't need anything besides food and whiskey.

"All business then, huh?" she said, then scurried off.

"I guess we *are* all business," Duggan said with a grin,

and nodded toward an empty table and chairs. "That do?"

"Fine," Slocum agreed. They could sit with their backs to the wall and see who came and went. The bar was full of boisterous dust-covered miners and teamsters. They hardly bothered to look up from their cards or drinks. Several girls were working the crowd.

Slocum dug out two cigars and offered one to Duggan. The man accepted, and Slocum struck a lucifer under the table. He held the flame out for Duggan to light his, then torched his own. Leaning back in the chair, he drew deep to let the smoke relax his still-rigid muscles. He watched one of the girls at the next table working a gray-whiskered man, who leaned forward talking softly to her.

Her small hand repeatedly patted his leg, and she nodded attentively to his words as they sat facing each other. Soiled doves could listen. They had a way that captivated men deprived of anything sweet-smelling or soft-skinned. They cared, or made their potential customers believe they cared. Many a man paid the full price just to sit there and talk with one of them. He never saw any more of her skin than what was exposed outside her dress under the flickering lamps. Never used her body, might never even lay a single finger on her, as if she was holy or his very own angel sent specially to listen to him—but he got his money's worth and more.

"I figure they'll get here tomorrow," Duggan said, pouring from the fresh bottle the bar girl delivered with two glasses.

"Could be. You know this country better than I do."

"I think they will be looking over their shoulder expecting us to come from back there, and they may even plan another ambush. That'll slow them down a lot. Besides, I don't figure they know the way well enough to ride up here without help."

"You mean they don't know your secret trail up here?" Slocum grinned at the man, and then shook his head in disbelief.

"By gawd, I got us here in one piece, didn't I?"

"You did that." He raised his glass to toast the notion that they'd made it, and they clinked glasses together and drank to their health.

Good whiskey. Slocum savored it as it cut the grit of the day from his mouth and throat. He sat back in his chair to enjoy the cigar and the liquor, watching the swish of dresses and petticoats as the girls plied their trade. He enjoyed females, and he really liked to watch them at work. Would that chubby brunette coax the next one she worked on into her crib out back?

He didn't have long to wait. Soon a lanky bear of a man with a gray beard down to his chest jumped up to his feet as if he were ten years younger, all pumped up with a new vigor. He danced a jig with his arm draped over the chubby one's shoulder. Then they headed for the curtained door at the rear. Slocum considered them with mild amusement as he looked over his glass. Then he sipped more of the rye, and as he savored it, looked for another bar girl in action.

"You have plans for that Arnold woman?" Duggan asked.

"No, we don't have any plans," he said with a shrug, then set his glass down and turned to the man. "You interested in her?"

"I could be. I've been thinking north somewhere, Colorado on the west slope. Hell, the Bighorn Mountains in Wyoming. I read they got most of the savages rounded up in that country. Man could get up where the bull elk still bugle. Still some silvertip bears left."

"You mentioned it to her?"

"I ain't half a hand at talking to women. Besides, why would she want to leave a good business and trade it for a string of packhorses and some ten-by-ten cabin made of lodgepoles built too short to stand up at the walls?"

"Maybe you should ask her sometime."

"You serious? You ain't joshing me?"

"Serious. Here comes our food."

"Damn, I was ready to order another meal. Figured I'd starve before it got here."

"Sorry, we're busy tonight," the bar girl said as she set down their heaping plates. "Gents, you need anything else?" Then she put her hands on the table, bending far enough over the table so both men could look down her blouse and see her small brown nipples.

"Looks good enough to me," Duggan said, armed with a fork and knife. "The food, that is."

"Thanks," Slocum said to her, and she left.

"You're serious?" Duggan repeated. "You and Hap haven't got a permanent thing in mind?"

Slocum shook his head. Two men came through the batwing doors and stopped under the lamps. He looked them over close. They wore high-crown hats and Coffeyville boots with their pants tucked in the tops. But neither man was familiar to him. He turned his attention to his food.

"I ain't digging in your life, but you ain't *only* looking for Flannery and the Kid, are you?" Duggan said between bites.

"A couple of bounty hunters," Slocum said, considering Duggan was safe enough to be told the truth.

"You tell me who they are when they come in. I'll send them camping on the next ridge."

"Thanks." Slocum shook his head. "But I can fight my own battles."

"I'll be that other arm until it gets well." Duggan punctuated his remarks with his fork.

He sounded serious, dead serious. Slocum hoped he didn't need his help, but he might. He never knew.

21

In the deep shadows of the big pines, Flannery could smell her musk. His arms were around her waist, and he held her to his chest, savoring his possession of her.

"That Tobin's stuck on you," he said under his breath.

"I guess so," she said dreamily, nuzzling her face on his shirtfront.

"How much would he pay?"

"Pay for what?" She lifted her face and blinked at him in the starlight.

"Dammit, for you to lay him."

"Oh, that. How should I know?" She shrugged.

"Girl, we're going to need all the money we can get our hands on if we buy us a high-class place up there at Globe. You slip up there and take him out in the woods. But I want you to get lots of money or lots of gold dust first before you let him touch you."

"Jesus, Flannery, I never was no damn crib girl," she whined in protest.

His fingers grasped her arms, and he closed his fingers tight enough that she drew in her breath.

"You sure were in heat last night with that damn Kid.

166

So it won't hurt to give this gent a tussle for some real money.''

'You knew about that?''

''Hell, you two made so much noise out there, you woke me up,'' he said under his breath.

''After you—''

''And another thing. Give me that sack of gold that old man gave you,'' he said sharply. ''I don't want you to lose it out there in the woods screwing Tobin.''

''I was going to buy me some new dresses with that,'' she protested.

''You'll have plenty of new dresses when we get to Globe.'' He jerked her up close with one hand, then reached in with the other and extracted the heavy pouch from between her breasts. ''Now go find him and get lots of money.'' He turned her in the direction of the camp, and then slapped her butt to send her on her way. She'd have to learn who was the boss sooner or later.

He watched her half stagger. Then she looked back as if for some relief. Impatiently he pointed in the direction he expected her to go. She shook her head wearily and then, in the pearly light, gathered her skirt and went toward the camp and Tobin.

The dumb Kid was already asleep in his bedroll. The previous night's activity and the long ride had worn his ass out. One thing the Kid must have done right. When he shot up that posse, it must have been a real good job. There had been no sign of them. And taking out that hunter had been a stroke of genius. Those miners would have lost the trail without Duggan. Flannery scrubbed his whisker-bristled mouth on his palm as he considered how much Lucy could earn.

Then he went back to their bedrolls. The Kid's snores were quiet enough. An owl hooted and made a silent flight over them as Flannery took a seat against a tree trunk and drank from his last bottle. Tobin said they'd be in Crown King at midday. A short ride left. Maybe they'd take a stage down to the foot of the mountains and then catch the one to Phoenix.

He took another swallow of the whiskey. He'd rest a damn sight easier when they reached Phoenix. He'd had his share of the Bradshaw Mountains. Damn Burns anyway. What had the miners done to him? He didn't want to think about it. If they tied Burns to him and the Kid and he didn't flush out of there in time, he'd have a new necktie. A hemp one. At least he'd tried to get Burns to leave. All that money Burns had—what would happen to it? He shook his head. Where did he keep it? *She knew.*

A plan began to spin in his mind. She was innocent. Miners courts never hung females. But she sure had run away with him and the Kid. That might look bad. But she could go back there and claim that she was Burns's wife and collect all his money.

How much did Burns have? Maybe there were thousands of dollars left. She would tell him how much when she got back. Where did Burns keep it? He took another nip of the bottle and stared at the stars that pricked the needle-layered ceiling. His new plan would buy him the best damn place in Globe. Crystal chandeliers, bartenders in formal coats, high-class whores upstairs, and gambling only for the rich. Once he'd been in such a place in St. Louis, and those bastards had hustled him out so fast he could hardly believe it. But he'd never forgotten the patterns on the green wallpaper and the two-story-tall drapes on the walls.

He was cold. He got up with some effort and jerked up a blanket to wrap up in. No telling how long that she'd be. He settled back to wait and think about his new palace. That would be the name—he'd call it the Palace.

He heard her coming, and raised up to watch her as she approached their camp. He hissed at her.

"Do any good?" he asked.

"Here," she said, and dropped several cartwheels on the ground.

"How much?" he asked, busy squirreling up the coins.

"I guess over fifty dollars. All he had on him." She stood over Flannery as if in a trance. He was on his hands and knees searching for any coins he might have missed. Then he looked up at her and frowned.

"What's the matter?" he asked.

"He offered to take me to San Francisco."

"He just liked your ass," Flannery said. The miner had never meant it. Hell, she knew how rich men lied to women like her.

"He never touched me," she said.

Flannery looked up in disbelief. His fingers clutched the money. What had she done for all this money?

"Was he a gelding?" he asked, blinking in disbelief.

"No, he was a gentleman." She folded her arms and looked away. "I told him I was in deep trouble because of my past company and I was trying to get away from it. That I needed money."

"Smart girl," he said, and climbed to his feet, jamming the money down in his pockets. Then he reached out, caught her arm, and spun her around so he could kiss her hard on the mouth. She'd do for a partner. His hand sought her breast and squeezed it.

"We're going to make lots of money together," he said, then sought her lips again.

In minutes, he had her on the blanket, legs parted, her dress shoved up and his pants undone. He crawled up, hastily stuck his aching manhood in her, and rushed to savor what he could. His breath grew short as he pounded her with his hips. The weight in his chest began to tighten, and he was forced to stop and gather more air.

Her fingernails dug into his flesh as she demanded that he respond.

"Dammit, don't quit now!" she cried in obvious desperation, raising her butt to capture him.

He lost his head and began to plunge into her with a newfound fury. Nothing would stop him, nothing. Then his world tilted and he knew he was about to pass out. His hips kept hinging like a bat-wing door in a strong wind. In and out he went without any letup, until the ache in his lungs grew so sharp, he thought a lance had been driven into his chest. An iron fist began to clutch his heart, and squeezed so hard he cried out as they both climaxed in a pile.

"Mick? Mick?" he heard her calling him from far away. The hurting in his upper body was so great, he couldn't move from where he lay on his side, holding his hands to his body and trying to survive the worst pain he had ever known.

He didn't know how long he had been passed out, but he knew it had been a while. It was still dark out, and he could see a few stars. With effort and some hard jolts, he managed to roll over on his back, swallowed hard, and then winced as the wave of hot bullets shot through his chest. What was wrong? This was the worst he had ever felt. He had to get off this mountain soon or he'd die on it.

"Can I get you a drink?" she asked.

"Yeah," he grunted, trying to get up, and fell back as she ran off. Whiskey might help, might ease the pain. The side of his face rested on the pine needles. He was still under the blankets. He decided to wait until she got back before he tried to sit up.

His vision was fuzzy, and he opened and closed his eyes repeatedly to clear it. Nothing helped. Light-headed. But it would clear up in few minutes. A swig of whiskey and he would be all right. Then he shut his eyes until tears escaped as another storm inside his rib cage exploded. The lightning ran down his arms, and he half fainted.

"I've got the whiskey," she said, sounding desperate and holding his head in her lap.

He tried to wake up. Couldn't clear his brain . . .

"Mick, Mick," she cried from afar.

22

"We better find us a place to sleep," Duggan said as they finished the last of the bottle of rye.

"Hell, I could just sit here forever and not wonder if I was going off over the damn edge of that mountain," Slocum said, feeling relaxed and content at long last.

"That damn mountain gets tougher every time I climb up it. I swear, I ain't going up it again unless my damn life depends on it. Are we going looking for them come dawn?"

"May as well. Sooner we get it over with, the better it suits me."

Duggan agreed with a tight-lipped nod, and they both rose to their feet.

"No women tonight?" the bar girl asked, coming over.

"Nope, but we may change our minds later," Duggan said with a grin. Then he reset his weathered four-peak hat on the back of his head.

"See you," Slocum said, and flipped her a two-bit tip.

"Any time, gents." And then she gave him a sly wink for his money and stuck the coin in her blouse.

The pair pushed out into the night. On the porch they

studied their jaded ponies, hipshot and sleeping. Slocum stepped off and undid his reins. He had started to step out to mount up when a familiar voice cut the night.

"Let's get us a drink and ask in here."

Two men were on horseback on the other side of Duggan's mount. They dismounted and walked past Duggan. Slocum kept his head down and backed the dun into the street using him for a shield. The Abbott brothers were in Crown King.

They disappeared through the bat-wing doors. Duggan frowned when Slocum waved him over.

"You know them," Duggan said.

"Yes."

"Is that the bounty hunters?" he whispered.

Slocum's gaze was still on the lighted doorway as the pair of louvered shutters still rocked from their passage. He gave a short nod. *Time for him to move on.* He mounted up with some effort. Things in his life had taken a new twist. Damn, all his good luck had all been used up coming up the mountain. He gave a nod to Duggan, the man nodded back, and they rode out of Crown King into the inky darkness.

Off to the side of the road, in a small clearing, they chose a camp, satisfied they were far enough away to catch some undisturbed sleep. Without words, they unsaddled, unfurled their blankets, and wrapped themselves up against the cold settling in. On the ground close by, Duggan raised his head.

"Them boys very tough?" Duggan asked.

"Tough enough."

"I guess you're kind of an expert on them?"

"They're tough."

"Are they going to find out you're up here?"

"I don't think so, unless someone sent them—say, from Owl Creek. They've got some picture posters that could be anyone. But they know me on sight. My own mother wouldn't know the picture, though."

"They ain't been to Owl Creek. You can't get up here

that fast unless you use that eagle-roost trail we took to-day.''

''Then they're just riding around and if they don't find me, they'll ride on.''

''I may make sure they do that,'' Duggan said. ''In the morning.''

''Don't mess with them.'' No need for Duggan to get mixed up with that grimy pair for his sake. He'd simply slip out of the Bradshaws.

''I'll handle it,'' Duggan said. ''Get some sleep.''

Nothing would change Duggan's mind. It was made up. Slocum closed his eyes and soon fell asleep. He awoke at the passage of some horses on the road. He listened for a long moment. There was the muffled sound of hooves on the ground; then they were gone. Had the brothers ridden past? Was it Flannery and the Kid? Who would know? Morning would come soon enough. He gathered the blanket over his shoulder, and then rolled over on his other side.

In the pre-dawn light, Duggan built an Indian fire in a small pit and boiled some coffee over it for them. The two sat huddled under their bedding for warmth and waited for the coffee, the smell growing stronger by the minute.

''You rest here,'' Duggan said. ''I'm going back to Crown King and send them boys headed for Prescott.''

''You figure you can fool them?''

Duggan scratched under the long hair behind his right ear. ''Yeah, I can send them packing. You watch the road and I'll be back in a few hours. I think we can have Flannery and the Kid caught before noon.''

''Someone rode by last night.''

''They went east. It wasn't them bounty hunters. I'd seen that white-blanket ass on the big one's Appaloosa in the starlight. Man, when we come out of that saloon and I seen it, I almost said out loud, 'Look, Slocum, someone's got one of them damn loud-colored Aps out here.' ''

''I'm glad you didn't.'' Slocum shared a grin.

"Hell, I didn't know that was them. I think we can scald ourselves on this coffee now," he said, and lifted the small pot with a kerchief for a holder.

The hot brew hit the spot, and after the second cup, Duggan saddled and rode back to Crown King. Slocum took his time saddling the dun, then let him graze, sat with his back to a trunk, and watched the noisy mockingbird flitting overhead. Using his wide tail for balance, the bird teetered back and forth on a bough.

In a short while, Duggan came back in at a trot. Slocum watched his backtrail with his Winchester as the big man dismounted.

"They're headed for Prescott. Left in a big hurry, fanning horseflesh and riding the wind for Iron Mountain and that way." He loosened the cinch to let his horse breathe, and then dropped to his haunches.

"What did you tell them?"

"I said I heard they were looking for a fella. They were asleep at the livery. I woke them up and I acted like I had come to get that big reward."

" 'You know where Slocum is?' they asked wide-eyed. Wish you could have seen their faces." Duggan slapped the side of his leg.

" 'Why, sure,' I said. 'Why, I drank whiskey with him on Prescott's Whiskey Row not two nights ago.' "

"They bought it?" Slocum asked in amused disbelief.

"They were saddling their horses while I kept asking them about that reward I had coming."

"What did they tell you?"

"They'd send it to me, and then they wasted no time in riding off."

Both men had a good laugh before they sobered. It was time to go get Flannery and the Kid rounded up.

"They ain't in Crown King yet?" Slocum asked.

"Nope, I'd a seen that paint horse."

"Unless he traded him off."

"Hell, he'd part with them bull-hide chaps of his before he'd give up on that paint."

Both men cinched up, and headed south on the faint road.

In two hours, they met a man driving a light wagon coming toward town.

"Howdy, mister," Duggan said in his big voice.

"Morning, gents," the man said, and reined up his horses.

"What have you got in that blanket?" Duggan asked with a nod toward it.

"A dead man. Died last night. Doc Hanks came up to our camp in the middle of the night to see about him. Seems he had him a heart stroke according to Doc. I guess to tell the truth, he was—well . . ." The man wiped his chin on the side of his hand. "I think he was, shall we say, with this pretty lady when his ticker blew up."

"Pretty lady, huh?" Duggan said, and dismounted. "I want a look at him, if it's all right."

"Sure. I got his name here. She wants it on his tombstone." The man fumbled in his pockets.

On his knees, in the bed of the wagon, Duggan undid the blanket, and then nodded to Slocum to join him.

"It's Flannery."

"That's his name on this paper." The driver waved it. "Mick Flannery."

"There was a kid riding a paint with him?" Duggan asked, covering up the blue-faced corpse.

"Oh, sure, he's back at our camp with that pretty girl. Guess she's this dead gent's widow. If you want her for yourself, though, you're probably too late. She's took up with that Tobin fella since this man of hers up and died on her."

"Who's Tobin?" Duggan asked.

"Some rich man's son." The driver shrugged as if he didn't know more than that. "They gave me the money to bury this gent and buy a tombstone."

"We better ride up there," Slocum said. "The Kid's up there."

Duggan agreed, and then shook his head as if in disbelief. "Flannery damn sure beat the hangman, didn't he?"

"Sure did, but sounds like he went out of this world enjoying himself." Slocum was amused at the notion as he swung his leg over his horse.

"Oh, he must have, gents," the driver said, and then clucked to his horses.

They turned and watched the man drive toward Crown King. Duggan turned back; he still looked amazed at the turn of events.

"I guess we all got to go someday," he said. "But damn, Flannery always looked the picture of health to me."

"And you can't tell when that call's coming," Slocum said as they put their horses into a trot.

"Just so they don't call us soon, pard." Then Duggan laughed aloud and spurred his horse into a lope.

23

"That damn Kid is shooting at us!" Duggan shouted, and drove his horse into the timber. Slocum and the dun were beside him as they plunged for the trees. The air buzzed like hornets with bullets. Wishing for an extra hand, Slocum drew the dun up short in the trees and then jumped from the saddle. He grasped the smooth wooden stock of the Winchester and jerked it from the scabbard. The long gun in his hand, he half crouched and looked to see which way his partner had gone.

He had seen the Kid in the road, trying to take aim from the back of his paint. Then he'd seen the muzzle smoke from the kid's rifle when Duggan shouted at him. He owed him. No accident—Duggan's cutting in front of him on the road had turned the dun the right direction in the nick of time.

Duggan hugged a tree a few yards away and was returning fire. Slocum joined him behind a nearby pine and pressed his back to the rough trunk.

"He wants to play games," Duggan said, shoving more cartridges in his rifle.

"I'll move to the right," Slocum said. "And we'll split his attention."

"No, I can move better than you can. You're lucky to handle that thing one-armed."

"Then I can empty my pistol at him and cover you."

"Good idea. I'd like to take him alive, since death cheated them boys back home from hanging Flannery."

"I agree—" Slocum's words were cut off by the barrage of bullets shredding bark on the tree beside him.

"Use your Colt, he's empty!" Duggan shouted.

Slocum stood the rifle up, then filled his left hand with the pistol grip and slung lead in the direction of the shots until the Colt hammer dropped on an empty round. By then, he knew Duggan was well up the hill. Slocum drew back, straightened up behind the tree, and stuck the pistol between his knees to reload it.

He heard Duggan cut down with his long gun, and the Kid let out a scream.

"You bastards done killed my horse!"

"You're next!" Duggan said flatly. "Throw up your hands or prepare to die!"

"I give up!"

"Throw your hands up!" Duggan ordered.

Slocum risked looking. He could not see anything but Duggan. He hefted the fresh-loaded .44 in his hand, and started forward at Duggan's wave to move in.

"You shot my horse. You killed him," the Kid cried on his knees. The paint was sprawled out on the ground.

"I wasn't aiming at him," Duggan said as he tossed aside the Kid's weapons, which lay on the ground. "I regret that, but you were standing right here and he was in the line of fire."

"You killed him," the Kid mumbled as Duggan jerked him up and tied his hands behind his back.

"I didn't do it on purpose." Duggan scowled at the Kid. "He got in the way."

"But you killed him—"

"Shut up!' "

Slocum went for their horses and brought them back.

"You reckon we got any business bringing the woman in?" Duggan asked.

Slocum shook his head. Duggan agreed, then loaded the muttering Kid on his own horse. He gave Slocum the reins, then stepped up behind Slocum on the dun.

"We'll get another mount for him in Crown King," he said.

Slocum looked back at the dead horse, and then nodded in agreement. One prisoner was going back. He would have to start thinking about his own next move. With the Abbots looking for him in Prescott, it made things tighter than he liked.

They reached Owl Creek on spent horses in a light mist of rain long past midnight. A crowd rushed out of the Silver King Saloon and appraised the captors and captive. Slocum dismounted, and caught the eye of his ex-partner, who was standing back on the porch holding his frock coat by the lapels.

"Interesting how *you got* your man," Markley said as Slocum drew up close. "And *they* never got *you*."

"You son of bitch, you sent them word where I was!" Slocum drove a fist into the man's gut. Markley gave a great gasp, and then bounced off the wall. He came back swinging. His fist caught Slocum's cheek.

Slocum cut Markley's jaw with an uppercut and snapped his teeth shut. The man stumbled back, spitting blood. So Markley had sent those two word about where they could find him. They had ridden into Crown King looking for him because Markley had sent them there.

In a flash Slocum had him by the front of his fancy shirt, jerking him half up. "I want my five hundred and fast."

"All right. All right." Markley struggled to his feet and staggered around unsteadily, holding his face. Not daring to take his eyes off Slocum, he backed through the swinging doors. Slocum stayed close, the rage making his chest swell as he followed Markley across the barroom.

"It's in the safe." Markley pointed, and his hand shook.

"Get it out. This isn't a robbery. You owe me that money from a saloon that you sold. That we both owned, and you skipped out with the proceeds."

"I tried to find you—"

"You knew where I was all the time. Get my money."

"Sure, sure."

"And don't go for no gun in that safe."

Slocum looked up and saw Christianson standing there, holding a long-barrel Peace Maker on Markley.

"Here," Markley said, slapping bundles of bills on the top of the safe.

"Count it," Slocum said.

With shaking hands, Markley began as his eyes shifted from Slocum to the Colt pointed at him.

"There's one hundred—there's two." He took the band off another bundle and continued counting, until at last he had counted out five hundred dollars.

"That will do," Slocum said, stepping in and gathering it up.

"I think, Mr. Markley, you need to hightail it out of here," Christianson said. "We ain't got a place for a cheater in this camp. You be gone at sunup if you know what's good for you."

"Huh? I never—I run this saloon." Markley blinked in disbelief.

"Too bad. They need a new man to run it. Don't be in this valley when the sun comes up." Christianson holstered his Colt.

"I can tell you that bastard's wanted!" Markley shouted. "I tell you there's a big reward on him. A thousand dollars! Slocum is a wanted killer!"

Slocum had reached the front doors. Then Markley went silent, and he turned to see why. Duggan held his great skinning knife at the man's throat.

"You tell one more lie tonight and you won't ever talk again."

"I . . . understand."

The customers in the place began to laugh. Slocum shoved the money down in his pocket and pushed out the door.

"The Kid's in jail," Christianson said as they hurried for Hap's place. "Up at the shack. I've got three guards. Do you plan to be here for his trial?"

"No. I better mosey on."

"Slocum, if I can ever help you . . . I was a lawyer once. Guess I'll go back to being one again. Can't find enough gold."

"Good luck, and thanks back there."

"No problem. Guess you're headed for her place?"

"Yes. I've got some unfinished business to take care of."

"Good luck."

Slocum was alone in the darkness. He hurried down the ruts. It was a shame to wake up a workingwoman this late. The thin mist veiled his face as he regretted his whiskers and lack of a bath. He must smell more like a horse than a human.

He saw the lamp in the tent, and hurried down to the flap.

"Welcome home. How is that arm?" Hap asked, rising from the bench.

"All right. Word must go fast."

"I came and woke her up," Mae said, coming in from the back of the tent, wearing the most respectable dress he'd ever seen her in.

'What was the ruckus down there?" Hap asked.

"Oh, I collected the money that Markley owed me."

"Well, you must be rich then," Mae said, looking at the ceiling and shaking her head in a knowing way. Both women laughed.

Duggan rushed in and swept off his hat at the sight of the two women.

"Mae, meet Sam Duggan, the best man you can ever ride with," Slocum said.

"Even up goat trails," Duggan added, and ducked down as if he feared being hit.

"Excuse me," Mae said to him, and turned back to Slocum. "I told Hap all about the Abbott brothers, and we agreed the best thing was for you to get out of the Arizona Territory."

"Now I have a mother," Slocum said, taking a cup of coffee from Hap, who next poured one for Duggan.

"Not a mother, but we all care for you. You can catch a stage at Prescott, take it to the railhead, and up there catch the Atlantic Pacific and be in Santa Fe in no time." Hap and Mae shared a nod of agreement.

"Only flaw is that Duggan sent the Abbot brothers to Prescott," Slocum said. "The Abbots will be coming back here to see Markley to find out where I went when they can't find me in Prescott. He's the one sent them the word."

"Running the sumbitch off ain't good enough," Duggan mumbled. "Wait, I've got a plan. You stay here till they come. Then we send them up that eagle trail to Crown King. They can't turn around and come back down until they get to the top, and by then you'll be gone. How does that sound?"

"They won't believe you a second time. It won't work."

"I ain't going to be the one tells them. You've got other friends in this town that will do it for me."

Slocum shook his head. "Sounds crazy to me."

"Face it, there are only two ways out of this valley. The road to Iron Mountain that goes on to Prescott, or this whatever he calls it," Hap said.

"Eagle's roost," Slocum said to her.

"Trust your friends," Duggan said, holding his cup out for more coffee.

"I'll take you out in a wagon after they start up that

mountain," Mae said. "Then even if they come back, they won't know how you left."

"You aren't staying here?" he asked.

"No. I'm going back east somewhere they don't know me and start me a millinery shop. I'm tired of this business."

"What about that fella with the fancy name? The Third?"

"Ha. He didn't know me the second trip up here."

"I see. And you?" he asked Hap.

"I think I'm tired of this business too. Guess I won't get rich here either. Two of them Chinese want to buy this place. They have the gold dust to buy it too."

"You ever seen the west side of the Rockies?" Duggan asked.

"No," she said, and blinked at him as if taken aback.

"I ain't making no indecent offer. I mean you and me. But I want to go see that country on the back side of them Rockies. There's supposed to be plenty of bull elk, trout in them streams, choke cherries by the bushels."

"Indecent offer?" Hap frowned at him as if amused.

"Well." He inhaled deep and his barrel chest swelled. "I know you got a man somewhere, ma'am."

"We ain't worried about that no-good." She dried her hands on the front of her dress and then squared her shoulders. "I'd like to see that side of the rockies, Mr. Duggan."

"Gawd a'mighty—yes—yes—soon as we get this boy safely out of here, I'll gather up a fine pony for you to ride. You know we can't take no fancy wagon. Packhorses is all that'll get back up there." He looked at her to be certain she knew the problems.

"I know."

"Since I'm not going to be using him, you can have the dun, Hap," Slocum said.

"Really?" Hap asked, taken aback again.

"Good, he's as surefooted as—a damn eagle," Duggan said. They all laughed.

• • •

They stood on the wooden platform. The sign overhead on the depot said, "Sante Fe Junction." Slocum looked over at the blue-green junipers that clustered the red-bouldered hillside. Mae wore the long conservative blue-plaid dress and matching bonnet as she stood before him. In his new brown broadcloth suit and beaver hat, he counted out three hundred dollars as they stood facing each other.

"What's the name of the town where you're starting this millinery business?" he asked.

"Rolla, Missouri. It's on the Frisco Line out of St. Louis," Mae said, wetting her lips. "I don't need your money."

"Yes, you do," he said, taking her hand and forcing the stack of bills into her fingers.

"Slocum, what will you do for money?" she asked, pained. Hurriedly she shoved the bills down in her matching drawstring purse.

"You say Rolla, Missouri, huh? It's on the Frisco line out of St. Louis, right?"

"Yes."

"I want you to run a good business there. I'll come by and check on you sometime."

"Promise me?"

He silenced her with a hard kiss on the mouth. Then he turned her around and with a small push sent her toward the train. She paused, undecided, and looked back. The conductor shouted, "All aboard!" Mae stared at Slocum, chewed on her lip, then hurried onto the coach.

He last saw her, her face at the coach window and throwing him kisses. He waved, and then when the last car was headed east, went down the platform and climbed in the first waiting rig.

"Going in to Santa Fe, *Señor*?" the driver asked.

"For a while, sir," he said, and drew out a cigar. "Are there any fandangos tonight in Santa Fe?"

"Oh, *Señor*," the driver said. "There are always fiestas and fandangos every night in Santa Fe."

"Good," Slocum said. He lit his new cigar and then settled back in the leather seat. He could already hear the music, see the pretty *señoritas* dancing and swaying to it.